Nathalia BUTTFACE

NIGEL SMITH has been a journalist, busker, TV comedy producer and script writer, winning an award for his BBC 4 radio comedy, *Vent*. More importantly, he has been – and still is – an embarrassing dad. Much like Nathalia Buttface, his three children are continually mortified by his ill-advised trousers, comedic hats, low-quality jokes, poorly chosen motor vehicles, unique sense of direction and unfortunate ukulele playing. Unlike his hero, Ivor Bumolé, he doesn't write Christmas cracker jokes for a living. Yet.

This is Nigel's fourth book about Nathalia Buttface.

Also by the author

Check out these great reviews from Lovereading4kids:

"One of the funniest books I've read." " *Abigail, age 11*

" I couldn't stop laughing." *Sam, age 10*

"The plot was hilarious and the ending was brilliant and unexpected." *Eloise Mae, age 11*

"I rate this book five stars because it is so funny and really cool."
Jenny, age 8

"This book is hilarious, amazing and gives me an embarrassing feeling on behalf of Nathalia!" *Elspeth, age 9*

"Nathalia Bumolé is one of the unluckiest kids ever, and most of it is her dad's fault!" *Elise Marie, age 9 ½*

"Makes me glad my dad is nothing like this dad, although he is still very embarrassing." *Emma, age 7*

Nathalia BUTTFACE

and the TOTALLY Embarrassing

Bridesmaid Disaster

BY

Nigel & Smith

Illustrated by Sarah Horne

HarperCollins *Children's Books*

First published in Great Britain by HarperCollins Children's Books in 2016
HarperCollins Children's Books is a division of HarperCollins*Publishers* Ltd,
HarperCollins *Publishers*, 1 London Bridge Street, London SE1 9GF

The HarperCollins Children's Books website address is
www.harpercollins.co.uk

1

Nathalia Buttface and the Totally Embarrassing Bridesmaid Disaster
Text copyright © Nigel Smith, 2016
Illustrations © Sarah Horne, 2016

Nigel Smith and Sarah Horne assert the moral right to be
identified as the author and illustrator of this work.

ISBN 978-0-00-816709-7

Printed and bound in England by
Clays Ltd, St Ives plc

To Michèle, for pretending I'm not as embarrassing as Dad.

And thank you to Ruth, for the awesome idea, the amazing editing and the annoying nagging about finishing the flipping book.

CHAPTER ONE

· · · ·

"DAD, I'M NOT COMING OUT OF THE CHANGING rooms and I'm not even joking and this wedding is utter pants and I hardly even *know* my lame cousin and bridesmaids are all rank and I LOOK TOTALLY STUPID and anyway I'm not doing it," said Nat.

Ever so loudly.

Dad looked at the sour-faced lady who ran DREAM BRIDES LTD – a hot and cramped little dress shop above a newsagents on the high street. He gave her what he hoped was a charming smile.

She wasn't charmed one little bit. Her face, which was stony to begin with, hardened to granite.

"She doesn't have to shout," said the lady, who was called Dolly Crumble and who was almost lost among the sickly pink and curdled cream and violently violet fluffy, frilly frocks that filled her little boutique.

"That's not shouting," said Dad, whose voice was muffled by some kind of purple velvet thing that was apparently a really important bit of a bridesmaid outfit and seemed to be attacking him. "When she was a baby and was hungry or had wet herself, THEN she shouted. You should have heard it."

"Shuddup, Dad," shouted Nat from the changing room. Billowing pink material surrounded her. It looked like she was being consumed by a possessed blancmange.

Dad didn't shuddup.

"When baby Nathalia started yelling in the car, people thought a fire engine was going past.

It was great – everyone else on the road got out of the way. I lost count of how many cars drove into lamp posts."

"Nobody cares, Dad," shouted Nat.

"Are you ready to come out yet?" asked Dolly Crumble. "Only you've been in there twenty minutes and this is the SIXTH Perfect Fairy Princess dress you have tried on."

"That's because they're all horrible," wailed Nat. "They all look like vomit."

"Such language," said the dressmaker, glaring at Dad as if he was to blame. "I hope she's going to be a better behaved young lady on the big day." She sniffed in a superior way and hoisted up her enormous bosom.

"A wedding is the most precious day in any woman's life. It is, you might say, the best moment of her entire life."

"Rubbish," said Nat. "There's tons of things better than a soppy wedding. There's getting to number one in the charts or winning Celebrity

All-Star Cook-Off or climbing Mount Everest or getting an Oscar or a Nobel Prize or an Olympic medal or going into space or—"

"Yes, well, not many girls will do those things," interrupted Dolly Crumble, "but all girls can get married."

"If everyone can do it, that doesn't make it very special then, does it?" argued Nat. There was a stony silence, like a big, gaping dark hole. Dad jumped into it. With both feet.

"Tell us about YOUR wedding day," he said. "If I've learned one thing in the last few weeks it's how much women like to talk about weddings. They really REALLY like to talk about weddings."

Nat thought she heard a rather strained tone in Dad's voice but as she was still being swallowed by the evil dress, she couldn't be sure.

The silence got EVEN worse.

"I have not had the pleasure of the bridal day," hissed the dressmaker. "Well, I had the pleasure of the DAY – the lovely church, the beautiful flowers, the glorious dress, the expectant relatives. What I did NOT have was the pleasure of Derek Sponge, my intended, turning up. No, he decided NOT to marry me, but to run off to Torquay to open a Bed and Breakfast with Sally Bucket, my next door neighbour."

"Oops," said Dad, stepping back. "You ready Nat?" he shouted. "We should be off soon."

"And so I vowed to make every other woman's day at the altar absolutely *perfect*, NO MATTER WHAT," said the jilted bride, "and whatever the bride wants, she gets. And *this* bride has left strict instructions that her six bridesmaids are to be six Perfect Fairy Princess Bridesmaids."

Angry little bits of spittle had gathered around MISS Crumble's top lip.

"And if it takes me all day to turn a turnip into a Perfect Fairy Princess Bridesmaid, then so be it!"

With that she whipped open the changing

room door and Nat popped out like a cork from a bottle of pink fizzy pop.

Miss Crumble picked up Nat and dusted her off.

"You're as beautiful as I can make you," she said. "Possibly as beautiful as ANYONE could make you."

"Thanks," snarled Nat.

Dad pushed the smothering purple material from his eyes. "Let's have a proper look at you," he said.

"This is my biggest and best Perfect Fairy Princess outfit. I call her the Esmerelda, the Flower Fairy Princess. Isn't she beautiful?" said the dressmaker, proudly.

"No, she's horrible," said Nat, miserably, "and I'm going to have to walk around in it ALL DAY including at the party afterwards when everyone else is in party clothes and having fun and being all cool. I'm going to look like a cross between Tinkerbell, a stick of candy floss and a sneeze."

Which is literally what she looked like.

Dad pushed the bit of purple material into his mouth for some reason. "No, it's all right actually," he said, squeakily.

Nat eyed him suspiciously.

His shoulders were shaking.

"Are you LAUGHING at me?" said Nat, furiously. "You are, I can tell, don't lie to me."

"It's nice to see you in a dress," coughed Dad in a strangled kind of way, "even a dress with big pink flowery wings."

"What even *is* this on my head?" snarled Nat. "It's got my hair all tangled up." Her long blonde hair was wrapped around some kind of pink fluffy crown. She tugged at it, but it was stuck fast.

"It's a tiara. All Perfect Fairy Princess Bridesmaids have to have tiaras, it's the law," said Miss Crumble, advancing towards Nat with a box full of sharp dress pins.

"What law?" snapped Nat.

"Fairyland law. Everyone knows that. Now, stand still and let me take it in. You haven't got a shape really, have you?"

"Dad, stop her talking about me like this," said Nat, "she'll make me sad."

"She's a professional," said Dad. "She's just got her…er… own dressmaking language."

"Ow, she jabbed me on purpose," yelped Nat.

"Of course I didn't," fibbed Miss Crumble.

Eventually, after much prodding and pushing and pinning and yelping, Dolly Crumble was satisfied and Nat and Dad were free to leave. Five minutes later they were sitting in the burger place opposite. Actually, Dad was sitting, Nat was hovering. Her bum was now a pincushion and it was too painful to sit.

Nat slurped her pop fiercely. So fiercely, in fact, that bubbles came out of her nose and made her even crosser. "Why have I got to be one of Tiffannee's stupid bridesmaids anyway, I hardly know her," she growled.

Dad sighed the sigh of a dad who has answered the same question six thousand times. Which was a bit unfair to Nat as he'd only been asked that question FIVE thousand times.

"You DO know Tiffannee. She's a close relative when you look at our family tree from a distance," he said.

"If you look at family trees at enough of a

distance, it looks like EVERYONE's related," said Nat, who had done evolution at school that term. "Everyone except Darius Bagley, who was made in a lab. By mistake."

Darius was not only the naughtiest boy in the history of schools ever, he was also Nat's best friend for reasons so old and complicated Nat couldn't even remember.

"But you are *properly* related to Tiff," said Dad. "She's the daughter of my cousin Raymonde. Auntie Daphne's son."

"Is she a proper Auntie or just one of those old women I have to call auntie even though they're not? The ones with hairy faces and a smell of cat wee?"

"Auntie Daphne is Bad News Nan's sister," explained Dad, patiently, "and you know Raymonde because he lives in Texas these days and always sends you baseball caps for Christmas."

"Oh yeah I like him," said Nat, who liked baseball caps.

"Tiffannee's his daughter, which makes her your, er, your, um—" Dad's eyes glazed over, "it makes her your relation anyway. Let's say cousin."

"I don't know why she can't get married in Texas," grumbled Nat, "we could all go there and eat cheeseburgers and get a tan and drive round in big cars."

"Tiffannee was born here, most of her relatives are here, and she says she's always dreamed of a perfect English wedding."

"I flipping well know THAT," said Nat, "it's all I've heard for months, Tiffannee's perfect wedding."

"I was pretty honoured to be asked to organise it," said Dad.

Nat snorted.

"I haven't really got the time," fibbed Dad, who always had loads of time, "but Raymonde's stuck out there in Texas working for that big oil company and, well, you can't say no to family."

Nat snorted again. "Tiffannee asked MUM to help organise her wedding, not you. No one would ask you to organise anything, not even a sock drawer. You write Christmas cracker jokes for a living and you don't even get those done in time."

Nat stamped her feet in silent fury as Dad just chuckled and dripped tomato sauce over his shirt. "I did do something useful actually," he said. "I got you promoted to THIRD ASSISTANT Bridesmaid. Cool, eh?"

"Brilliant, thanks," grumbled Nat sarcastically as they clambered into Dad's rubbish old campervan, the Atomic Dustbin. The Dog licked Nat's face, as if to say he understood her fairy princess pain. As they drove off in the familiar cloud of black engine smoke, Nat's brain was working overtime.

I'm not doing it, she thought. *I don't care how I get out of it, but I'm not doing it. I just need a plan...*

CHAPTER TWO

. . . .

At HOME THERE WAS NO ESCAPE FROM THE wedding horror.

The kitchen table – and indeed most of the house – was covered in silly wedding magazines. They were stuffed with glossy photos of daft looking, super-skinny, soppy brides pouting smugly on beaches, or draped over park benches, like they were homeless.

"Do you think if we spoke to Tiffannee she might change her mind about fairy princesses and have a less ridiculous wedding?" asked Mum, as she sat in the kitchen, listening to Nat's woes.

"She seems pretty set on fairies," said Dad. "She wants a Fairytale Wedding, and so fairies are important."

"And no one says no to a bride, apparently," muttered Mum with half an eye on her mobile phone, "even one who demands really mad things."

Nat snorted. "Who even likes fairy princesses? It's like that lame school play we did last term."

Nat had played keyboards in the school orchestra for their production of *A Midsummer Night's Dream*. She'd thought it was totally pants and soppy and it had only been enjoyable at all because Darius had jammed the smoke machine full on and the fire brigade had had to be called out.

A horrible thought struck Nat and she gasped.

"You took pictures of that play," she said, "and you sent them to all the family! OMG, Dad, it's YOUR FAULT. *You've* given Tiffannee the stupid idea to have a stupid fairy wedding. Which makes you – stupid."

Mum crossed her arms and looked at Dad, a small smile playing around her mouth. "I hadn't thought of that," she said, "your father is a buffoon sometimes."

Dad looked guilty. Nat wanted to strangle him.

"Still, I suppose we should be grateful Dad didn't send her pictures of *The Wizard of Oz*," said Mum, "or she'd be making the bridesmaids into munchkins."

"And Dad would be the scarecrow," said Nat, "the one without a brain."

"Cooee! Only me," said Bad News Nan, bustling into the kitchen with two enormous carrier bags. "Ooh, I'm starving. My stomach thinks my throat's been cut."

Mum slipped quietly out of the kitchen as Bad News Nan plonked herself down and took a packet of biscuits out of a bag.

"I'll have to have them dry as no one's offered me a cup of tea yet," she said, taking her false teeth from her pocket and popping them in her mouth.

"Nan, can you help me get out of being a stupid Perfect Fairy Princess Bridesmaid?" said Nat, making tea.

"Certainly not," said Bad News Nan, "you can't back out of being a bridesmaid, oooh the very thought. If your auntie Daphne was dead she'd turn in her grave."

Nat thought she heard Mum giggling in the living room.

"We'd never hear the end of it, you letting the family down. Your uncle Cuthbert let the family down and it killed him."

"Mum, Uncle Cuthbert lived to be a hundred and six," said Dad, "he was the oldest Bumole in history."

"And the wrinkliest," shouted Mum from the living room.

"I tell you it killed him stone dead," said Bad News Nan, living up to her nickname. "He promised to save that big tinned Christmas pudding for everyone – but he couldn't wait, could he? Boiled it up on Christmas Eve, forgot to put a hole in the tin and BOOM! Only person ever to be killed by a flying plum pud."

"Yeah, since you put it that way, you've got a point, Nan," sniggered Nat squeakily.

For some reason, even though Bad News Nan only ever knew horrible, miserable, doom-laden, *awful* news, she always cheered Nat up. Maybe it was because her nan enjoyed the bad news so much.

"Plus another thing," Bad News Nan droned on, "your auntie Daphne won't stop talking about what a big shot Raymonde is, over in America. Multi-billionaire she says he is, just cause he bought her a caravan at Camber Sands. So you, young lady, are not going to show us up."

Nat sighed.

"Besides," Nan continued, from behind a shower of biscuit crumbs, "you should think yourself lucky you're going to a wedding at all. All I ever get invited to is funerals."

"You *like* funerals," said Dad. "You even go to funerals of people you've never met."

"I like to keep up," said BNN, "they give me ideas for mine. And there's always a good spread afterwards. There was half a side of ham left over at Doreen Wilmore's wake last week. It just fit in my shopping bag. Kept me in sandwiches for days," she added, smacking her lips.

Mum popped her head around the door. "Gotta dash," she said. "I promised to run Tiffannee to the Castle where she's having the reception. There's some kind of issue over the buffet. It might even be a crisis."

"Castle?" said BNN. "Castle, oooh that is posh. Ideas above her station, people will say. Not me, of course. But it is a bit flash."

"It's the Castle Court Hotel and Country Golf Club," said Dad patiently. "You know this, you've got an invite. After the church, we're going there to have lunch, and then there's a band and disco."

"And fairy princesses," growled Nat. "Let's not forget the fairy princesses."

"I got my wedding outfit from the charity shop today," said Bad News Nan, taking a huge, bright green dress out of a shopper. She stood up and pulled it on over her clothes.

"What do you think?" she said. "As it's supposed to be a fairytale wedding, I was going for a 'Queen of the May' look."

Queen of the Swamp, more like, thought Nat. Bad News Nan looked like a massive lump of snot, wrapped in pond slime.

"It's different," said Dad, stuffing a hanky in his mouth for some reason.

"Oh please, Daddy, is there any way I can get out of being a Perfect Fairy Princess Bridesmaid?"

pleaded Nat in her best – in other words, most pathetic – voice.

"Well," said soft Dad, wilting like Superman in a Kryptonite onesie, "not really, love. Oh stop making that face."

"It's Tiffannee's big day," said Bad News Nan, "and brides get what they want. Not like funerals. You're at the mercy of the living. I've asked for six black horses and a Viking longboat but your dad won't organise it, I know."

Sniff, went Nat.

"If you didn't do it, it would be bad luck and might cause family upsets for years to come," said Dad, trying not to look at her.

Sniff, went Nat. Big fake tears plopped on to her jeans as she fixed her doleful eyes on Dad, who hid behind Nan.

"People get written out of wills," said Dad.

"You might get an oil well one day," said Bad News Nan, "his mum got a caravan, remember?"

"You'd like an oil well, wouldn't you?" said Dad.

"Don't care, not worth it," wailed Nat, plonking herself down in misery and chucking six copies of *PERFECT BRIDE MAGAZINE* on the floor.

Nat was sure Dad was weakening when her dramatics were rudely interrupted by the doorbell, followed by a young woman's voice shouting shrilly, "Ding dong wedding bells!"

It was blushing bride-to-be Tiffannee, with her usual – and annoying – greeting.

"Do you remember, before she moved to Texas and decided to become American, how she used to be called Rosie?" Nat whispered to Bad News Nan.

"Course," said Bad News Nan, "Rosie Lee Jones. She was a pudgy little thing with brown frizzy hair and teeth like wonky tombstones."

"She was also a lot nicer though," said Nat, quietly.

The woman that now greeted them was

NOTHING like the old Rosie.

Tiffannee was stick-thin and nut-brown, with bright blonde hair and bright blue eyes and a perfect, dazzling, super-white smile. Her pastel yellow summer dress was short and stylish and wrinkle-free. She rushed to hug Nat but stopped just as she got there.

"Don't want to wrinkle the dress!" she said. "Air kiss, air kiss!"

She smoothed her dress out, just in case the air had wrinkled it.

"It's one of Diana De Milano's," she said proudly.

"Have you borrowed it off her?" said Nat.

"She's a very famous designer," said Tiffannee, laughing. "She's doing my fairytale wedding gown too, don't you remember?"

Nat didn't remember, because she didn't care.

While Tiffannee went off to talk to Mum, Nat turned angrily to Dad. "I'm telling her I'm not doing it and you can't stop me. I'm not gonna be in a bazillion family photos dressed like a ridiculous fairy princess with MASSIVE butterfly wings and a spangly tiara. I look like something even hobbits would make fun of.

Suddenly Mum dashed back in. "I just need my purse then we're off," she said. Nat stood up.

"This bridesmaid thing—" began Nat, summoning up her courage to say she wasn't going to do it, no way no how, no ifs or buts.

"Oh yes, I forgot to tell you, good news – Tiffannee's arranged for all her bridesmaids to go to a spa tomorrow!" said Mum.

"Spa?" said Nat.

"Yes," said Tiffannee, coming back in, "that really a-maze-balls one that was in the paper. I want you all to get pampered and massaged and made-up and everything. The works, treat yourselves. It's my little thank you to my fairy princesses."

Nat paused.

"I'm so jealous," said Mum. "It's supposed to

be a wonderful spa."

Nat paused a bit more.

"Now, what were you saying about the bridesmaids?" said Dad.

"Nothing important," said Nat.

"I think it was," said Dad, helpfully.

"Shuddup, Dad," said Nat firmly, "it definitely wasn't important."

I'll get out of being a bridesmaid tomorrow, thought Evil Nat, who was always lurking somewhere in a grubby corner of Nathalia's brain. *AFTER the a-maze-balls spa...*

CHAPTER THREE

· · · ·

THE NEXT DAY WAS A LOVELY SPRING DAY, SUNNY and warm. Nat hopped cheerily on to the minibus that was to take her and Tiffannee's five other bridesmaids to the FABULOUS YOU! spa.

Nice one, Nat, she thought to herself. She walked smugly down to the end of the bus where the other five bridesmaids were waiting.

Like Tiffannee, the other bridesmaids were about ten years older than Nat. It was exciting to get to hang out with grown-ups. Even better, as Nat walked towards them, she could hear the other girls already hating on someone. Nat was looking forward to hearing all the wedding gossip while hopefully getting sparkly nail varnish on her toes.

"...little miss perfect, the *pet* fairy," said the Chief Bridesmaid, who was called Daisy Wetwipe. She had a butterfly tattoo on her shoulder and a sharp nose that pointed upwards.

Oooh, thought Nat, *girls are so mean! I wonder who they've got it in for. At least for once it can't be me as they don't even know me. This is waaay better than school.*

"*I* should have been Third Assistant Bridesmaid," said a girl with scraped back blonde hair called Tilly Saddle. Her hair was so tightly yanked back it pulled her eyelids up into a look of permanent shock.

"Yes, you should. Or me, at any rate. And now she's taken that place, which *should* have been either me or you," sniffed Erin Granule, who had a little moustache.

"She's trying to climb the bridesmaid ladder," said Annie Chicken, who exhibited a nose stud which looked like a fat spot.

"*You're* in danger now of course, 'cos you're *Second* Assistant Bridesmaid," said Daisy to a girl called Bella Drench, who had black frizzy hair piled up like a loo brush, and had shaved her eyebrows and drawn them back on.

"Yes, she'll be after your place next."

"Not if we get her first," whispered Bella, her eyes flicking darkly in Nat's direction as she sat down next to them.

"Hi, I'm Nat, who we hating on?" said Nat, a little nervously.

Five pairs of bridesmaid eyes glinted angrily at her.

That would be me then, thought Nat, sliding down into her seat, *it IS just like school, after all.*

After a tense and embarrassing journey, with Nat catching regular unpleasant whispers behind her, the minibus at last pulled into a wide gravel drive that cut through beautiful green lawns.

They parked alongside a large number of big shiny cars in front of a huge old house. The house reminded Nat of a Victorian school. *Or perhaps a Victorian prison*, she suddenly thought, as she saw a bunch of people in grey tracksuits being marched up a hill and made to do press-ups.

That doesn't look very relaxing, thought Nat. Then she noticed a big sign.

The full name of the spa was:

FABULOUS YOU!
SPA, WELLNESS AND
FITNESS... FOREVER.

Underneath, someone had painted the words:

OR ELSE.

Which alarmed Nat a little.

The bridesmaids were greeted at the front door by a trim woman in a blue tunic with thin lips and a clipboard. She had one of those tight smiles that people who don't enjoy smiling have.

Her plastic name badge read:

Gertie Catflap.

"Welcome to your super fun-packed luxury spa day," said Ms Catflap, handing each of the girls a form.

"Sign this, it means we're not responsible if

anything happens to you during a treatment."

As they signed, she said: "The changing rooms are on the left. Please get into your swimming costumes. Quick as you like now, you don't want to miss a fun-packed minute. Go, hurry."

Her smile got tired about halfway through, so by the time she said 'fun-packed' it looked like she was sending them all down for a ten stretch in the clink. Nat didn't want to think about what Ms Catflap would do to anyone who DIDN'T have a super fun-packed time.

None of the other bridesmaids spoke to Nat in the changing rooms.

Be like that, Nat thought. *I'll just have a day of pampering on my own. See if I care.*

She put on her bathing cossie and wrapped a fluffy spa robe around herself. She wished Penny Posnitch was here to enjoy it with her. She smiled and thought how much fun she'd have telling her friend all about her super fun-packed luxury spa day at school tomorrow.

Obviously she wouldn't bother telling her friend Darius about it, because his idea of a super fun-packed day would probably involve tactical nuclear weaponry and a big red button.

The first treatment was in a large, brick-lined room, built around a massive mud bath. Gentle music was piped in from somewhere. The lighting was soft. The mud, however, smelled like farts.

Actually Darius WOULD like this, thought Nat.

The girls clambered into the big tub filled with the warm, gloopy mud. Close up, the mud smelt of perfume that didn't QUITE mask the smell of rotten eggs.

Nat sank into the muck with a big, ploppy, trumpety noise.

"Hey, it wasn't me," she said, as the other bridesmaids pulled faces.

"Now ladies, you must wear shower caps," said Gertie Catflap, popping her head round the door. "If this mud gets in your hair it'll *never* come out," she said, before disappearing again.

But just as Nat reached for a plastic cap, she felt someone's leg slide sneakily around the back of hers...

And give it a deliberate, hard yank.

Before she could even yell, Nat was tipped right over and landed with a squelch, face-first in the sticky, stinky mud.

"Blech, you flup glupp cowpig," Nat coughed, coming up for air. "You did that on purpose. Who was it?"

The other bridesmaids just laughed nastily and pretended to look innocent.

"It's very slippy in here, little girl," said Second Assistant Bridesmaid Bella Drench, who Nat reckoned had definitely done it.

"It's dangerous, getting pampered," said Tilly Saddle smugly.

"You might be better off sitting back in the minibus with some crisps and a fizzy drink," simpered Erin, who had a tiny fleck of mud stuck on the end of a moustache hair.

"Nothing too greasy though… " said Annie Chicken, nose stud quivering meanly.

"No, she doesn't want to get MORE spots, does she?" cackled Daisy, as the others all joined in the laughter.

Not for the first time in her life, Nat wished Darius was lurking nearby. He might be a tiny evil ninja of doom, but he was HER tiny evil ninja of doom, and that's just what this rotten lot needs, thought Nat, pulling lumps of sour-smelling mud from her hair and spitting great gobs of it back into the bath.

"Ew," said the bridesmaids.

"Shuddup," said Nat, in her best Darius/evil ninja of doom voice.

"Hardly perfect Third Assistant Fairy Princess Bridesmaid behaviour," said Daisy, sharply.

"I don't care," snarled Nat. "I never wanted to be Third Assistant Fairy Princess Bridesmaid anyway…" she began.

"I told you!" said Daisy, looking at the others. "She wants to be *Second* Assistant Fairy Princess Bridesmaid."

"Don't be ridiculous," said Nat.

"No, she wants to be *Chief* Fairy Princess Bridesmaid!" said Tilly Saddle, gasping in horror.

"You're bonkers," said Nat, "and more than that, you're all a bunch of—"

"OK girls," interrupted Gertie Catflap as she burst back into the room, "time to get showered off. Follow me."

Nat and the other bridesmaids were led to a small shower room decorated all over with blue and white shiny, tiny tiles. But instead of the usual shower nozzles on the walls, there was just one great big hose.

"This is a high-pressure hose," said Gertie Catflap, "to help get all that sticky mud off. It is quite powerful though, so you do have to be careful. Do you want me to hose you down, or would it be more super-fun to do it yourselves?"

"Oooh let us, we just *love* super fun, don't we girls?" said Daisy, grabbing the hose.

"No, can you do it?" said Nat, who didn't like Daisy's tone.

"All right, you can do it," said Gertie Catflap not hearing Nat, "but do be careful, it's very high pressure. Don't go mad!" She closed the tiled door behind her.

"Of course," said Daisy Wetwipe. "I'm not mad…"

She grinned at Nat.

"I'm furious," she whispered.

CHAPTER FOUR

· · · ·

"I'M ACTUALLY QUITE CLEAN," SAID NAT, SCRAPING bits of drying mud off herself as she tried to make a break for the door but discovered her knees were locked together with gloop.

Daisy was way too fast. Nat was backed against the wall as the Chief Bridesmaid pointed the hose at her and the other girls gathered round on all sides, hemming her in. With an evil grin, Daisy began to turn the big metal wheel with 'WATER PRESSURE' written on it, twisting it right round to:

FULL POWER – ONLY TO BE USED BY EXPERIENCED STAFF.

The other bridesmaids snickered as Nat looked frantically around the small room, trying to escape. But there was nowhere to hide.

"Enjoy your shower, you little creep," said Daisy, and pressed the ON switch.

For a long moment nothing happened except a horrid gurgling noise, deep in the pipes. The hose trembled as the pressure built up.

"I'm gonna spray you to kingdom come," cackled Daisy, gripping the hose tightly with both hands.

And then the water shot out like a rocket.

Now, Nat had done rockets at school, and Darius liked building them, so she was a bit less surprised than Daisy by what happened next. Instead of the water lifting *Nat* off her feet and shooting her across the shower room, the OPPOSITE happened.

"Aaaargh! Help!" squealed Daisy, as she was hurled into the air by the power of the water, shooting out of the wildly bucking hose.

"Waaaah!" she screamed as she was shot around the room in a big circle, sliding across the walls, like one of those motorbike riders on

the wall of death at the circus.

"Let go!" shouted Bella.

"I can't! I'm too scared!"
shouted Daisy, the pressure
lifting her six feet off the
ground. "Turn it off, turn it off!"

She was now whizzing around at the top of
the room, and gathering speed all the time.

"The wheel's jammed!" squealed Annie
Chicken, frantically trying to turn it off.

"You're turning it the wrong way!" shouted Tilly.

"Now it IS stuck!" squealed Bella. "You
absolute idiot – blaaaagh!"

The last noise was because she got hit, smack-bang in the mouth, by the water.

"I'm drowning!" shrieked Bella.

"If you were drowning, you couldn't speak," cackled Nat, dodging the watery jet. She was quite enjoying herself now.

Suddenly, Bella's loo-brush hair shot off in a big black frizzy mass. She shrieked even louder. "My hair extension! That cost me a fortune. Someone grab it before it goes down the drain…"

All hell broke loose. Two bridesmaids tried to grab the flying Daisy, Annie struggled with the wheel and Bella scrabbled after her disappearing hair, which slithered towards the drain like a big soggy spider getting flushed down the loo.

Nat realised that all the spray had sloshed her clean as a whistle and she could move again. She saw her chance and dashed for the exit.

She slipped through and slammed it behind her in relief.

"Everything all right?" said Gertie, who had

come over to check on the faint wails and squeals that were coming from behind the door.

"Very all right," said Nat.

"Are you sure? I thought I heard screaming and the words: 'HELP, HELP, I'm going to die'."

"Oh, you know us bridesmaids," said Nat. "We do like to scream. It's all the excitement, waiting for the big day."

Just then, the door burst open and Bella came hurtling through it, gripping her sodden, ruined hair extensions. She skidded on the floor like a rocket-powered fish and lay, panting, at Nat's feet.

"You… you…" said Bella, pointing at Nat and coughing up water. "You are responsible…"

"For all the fun and good bridesmaid times? Too kind," said Nat. She grabbed a nearby towel and began to help dry Bella off, making very sure she shoved the towel in her face, really firmly.

"You're wiping my eyebrows off you little— mumph," said Bella, but her words were muffled by the fluffy towel.

"Lovely spa you've got," shouted Nat to Gertie, rubbing even harder.

"Gerroff!" said Bella.

Behind them, the wailing slowed down and eventually stopped.

The Second Assistant Fairy Princess Bridesmaid, now with short hair and no eyebrows, grabbed the towel and flung it across the floor. "I give up," she said, bursting into tears. "Take my place! I can't win. You are a bridesmaid MONSTER."

With that, she ran off to the changing rooms.

The door to the shower room opened once more. Nat felt the glares of Tiffannee's remaining fairy princesses boring into her back like hot fairy knives.

The rest of the spa day was just as horrid. Nat tried to talk to the other bridesmaids and tell them she wasn't ACTUALLY trying to nobble them all, but they refused to listen. In fact, they all kept their distance, jumping a mile every time she tried to say anything. They looked at her the way very tasty gazelles look at very hungry lions.

The only reason Nat didn't get more upset about the horrid bridesmaids was that she was kept too busy to think much about them. The rest of the day wasn't so much a relaxing pampering spa experience – with warm fluffy towels and hot oils and foot rubs and gentle eyebrow-shaping – as a *terrifying boot camp of pain.*

Instead of glittery toenail painting she got the EXTREME ZUMBA POWER HOUR which made every muscle ache. And instead of a gentle massage she got OLGA THE PUMMELER who found those muscles and pounded them into weeping submission. Then there was a JOG AND SWEAT DETOX session in a big damp plastic suit and finally she had to drink a huge glass of HEALTHY HELGA'S CLEAN IT OUT NOW! JUICE. And all under the silent evil glare of the other fairy princesses, who weren't QUITE pummelled and sweaty and detoxed enough to forget to glare.

It was miserable. She was glad when it was all over and the minibus dropped her home again.

"I thought you'd gone to get de-stressed," said Dad as she barged through the door and up to her room, "you look ten times worse!"

CHAPTER FIVE

. . . .

IN SCHOOL THE NEXT DAY, NAT TOLD PENNY POSNITCH her latest troubles, recounting the spa story in full gory detail.

"That's funny," chuckled Penny, not very helpfully.

"That's not helpful."

"I suppose those bridesmaids do sound horrible, but I don't see what your problem with fairies is," said Penny.

"That's because you LIKE fairies," said Nat. "What did you hand in last week instead of your history homework?"

"Pictures of fairies," said Penny, "but that's better than Darius, who drew a picture of his—"

"I know exactly what he drew a picture of," snapped Nat, "that's why he's been sitting in the corridor for every history lesson since."

Nat sighed a big sigh. "How do I get out of this wedding?"

"My dad says there's only one way to get out of a wedding," said Penny.

"What is it, *what is it*?" said Nat, hope flaring briefly, like a flame in the darkness of her soul.

"If you were already invited to *someone else's* wedding," said Penny.

Nat sighed again. The tiny flame of hope had turned out to be a mega meteorite of doom.

What a daft thing to say, Nat thought. *What are the chances of getting invited to someone else's wedding on the same weekend at such short notice?*

Suddenly, she smelt something damp and

earthy. Then she felt a wriggling beside her and noticed Darius was sitting next to her, picking his nose and eating it.

"Were you doing sneaky listening, chimpy?" said Nat.

Darius just shrugged.

Nat thought he had that strange look on his face that meant one of two things. One, he could be thinking deeply. Or two, he was going to burp the alphabet. Both always ended badly.

She took a gamble and hoped that he was thinking the slightly less disgusting option.

"Get me out of this wedding," she said. "I know you can. I'm the only person in the world who knows you're actually a tiny evil genius and not just a chimp."

"What do I get?" said Darius, looking across the school playground. The sky had darkened.

"I'll owe you a favour," said Nat, feeling like she was doing the sort of deal people warn you never to do.

"What sort of favour?" There was a clap of thunder and rainclouds gathered overhead.

"I dunno, whatever you want," said Nat.

Lightning hit a church steeple over in the distance.

"Deal," said Darius, spitting on his hands.

Nat took a deep breath and took his disgusting, squishy hand.

They shook on the deal.

Darius smiled an evil smile.

"So, what do I do?" asked Nat.

"OK, the first thing you have to do is pretend you REALLY wanna be a bridesmaid. Agree to anything the stupid bride wants you to do."

"That's bonkers."

"Nah, it just means she won't suspect anything when you DO get out of it."

"Sneaky," said Nat.

"I'll also have to meet this Tiffannee," said Darius, "see how tricky it's gonna be."

"Sure," said Nat, "come round on Saturday."

Darius smiled and offered her some earwax.

"I get bored with just bogeys," he said.

Not for the first time, Nat wondered if Darius was a genius who pretended to be a chimp, or if it was the other way round.

Nat's Saturday morning lie-in was broken by the sounds of clanging and banging and shouting from downstairs. She wandered crossly down to the kitchen to find Mum telling Dad off (the shouting) and Darius hunting for food in the pantry (all the other noises).

"There's only three weeks to go to this wedding and you haven't even ordered Tiffannee's centrepieces," said Mum. "You're meant to be helping me, remember?!" Dad was looking at a list Mum had written for him with TO DO – URGENT on it.

NOTHING was ticked off.

Except Mum. Mum was really ticked off.

"Two things in my defence," said Dad, taking a nervous gulp of tea. "One is that I was a bit late on finishing off those Christmas cracker jokes, and had to do those first, and two…" he paused, "I don't actually know what centrepieces ARE."

Mum told Dad EXACTLY what they were in great detail and with some rude words chucked in too. Nat chuckled and jabbed Darius in the backside with a fork.

"Stop that," she snapped, "you're supposed to be working on a great plan to get me out of this. If your great plan is just to come round and stuff your fat face then our deal is off."

He retreated out of the pantry with a loaf of bread and a pot of jam.

"Wedding bells, ding dong!" trilled Tiffannee, at the door.

She rushed into the kitchen, air-kissed Nat and then noticed grubby, twitchy Darius. He put his face out for an air kiss. Jammy splodges dripped off it. Tiffannee stepped back in alarm.

"You must be Darius. I've heard a lot about you," she said backing away. Nat thought her face seemed to say: *Enough to keep well out of your way.*

"He's a bit sticky, but he's generally harmless," said Nat. She thought for a moment. "Well, he's nowhere near as bad as everyone says."

Then Tiffannee told them all – in full dull detail – about a row she'd had with her aunt. She was staying with Auntie Daphne until the wedding, but she was quite moany about her.

"She insists on bringing me TEA in bed every morning," complained Tiffannee, "and I've told her, we drink COFFEE in Texas."

Mum looked a bit disapproving.

"Of course then I realised I was being silly," said Tiffannee.

Mum smiled.

"I mean, I CAN'T drink coffee, my teeth

need to be super-white for my wedding," the bride-to-be went on.

Mum frowned again. "Tiffannee," she said, "I know you want things to be perfect, but you're going to drive yourself doo-lally."

Along with the rest of us, thought Nat.

Tiffannee looked at a big gold watch on her wrist and squealed: "OMG, we have to go. Hiram's meeting us in town. Said he wants to see where I grew up."

"I'm not sure she HAS grown up," said Mum once Tiffannee had dashed off.

"Come on, Darius, get out of the pantry," said Nat as they all trooped off, adding wickedly, "oh and please make sure you sit next to lovely Tiffannee in the car."

Mum waved them all off at the door. She said that *unfortunately* she was "too busy with work" to come. But Nat caught a sneaky peek at her laptop, and there was definitely a movie on it, not a spreadsheet.

The lucky groom who was marrying their English rose was a Mr Hiram J Wartburger III.

He was waiting for them in a busy café just off the shopping centre.

The Texan oilman was big and rectangular like an oak wardrobe. He had an enormous square chin and a bald spot bigger than Dad's. He was wearing a bright, candy-stripe suit, which made him look like an oversized stick of rock.

He stood up when they came into the café and in a huge booming voice said: "Hey! Over here! Over here! Can you see me?"

"We can't really miss you in that suit," said Dad.

"Mighty pleased to meet you all," said the man as they sat down. "Hiram's my name, hire 'em and fire 'em, that's mah game."

He said that very loudly and very proudly.

"Sorry?" said Dad.

"What ah mean is, ah say I hire people, and then if they get uppity, ah fire them, just like that." He snapped his fingers. "Now what do you think of that?"

"What do you mean by 'uppity'?" asked Dad, scanning the plastic menu.

"Like asking too many questions," said Hiram looking at Dad, then breaking into a huge grin which showed his enormous, bright white teeth, "that's uppity. Like that one you just asked. You would now be fired! Yes, sir."

Tiffannee giggled.

"Take no notice of the big lunk," she said, "he's all talk, he's a total pussycat really."

"Ah confess ah'm as nervous as a fire-eater on an oil rig, that's for sure," said Hiram, "I mean, meeting you folks and all, I want to make a good impression on mah new family."

By now, customers in the café were turning round to see what the noise was. One elderly woman with blue hair tutted and her husband briefly looked up from his meat pie and said, "It's all right, dear, I think he's *American*."

He said the word *American* in a kind of whisper, as if he was naming an embarrassing medical problem, like a bumrash that might be catching.

"Oooh, that explains it," said the blue-haired old lady, "poor thing. I suppose they have to shout because their country is so big. Hard to hear each other, maybe."

Nat felt herself growing more and more

uncomfortable as Hiram told them how EVERYTHING was bigger, faster and better in Texas than anywhere in the world, especially "little old England".

Tiffannee gave him peck after peck on the cheek – aaargh thought Nat, public display of affection urgh.

"Isn't he AMAZING?" whispered Tiffannee to Nat eventually. "Isn't he just the bee's knees and the cat's pyjamas rolled into one?"

"He certainly thinks so," muttered Darius. Nat hid a giggle.

The waitress came over with a bacon sandwich for Hiram, who looked at it, and seemed confused. "Excuse me, miss," he said loudly to the waitress, who was young and spotty and bored.

"Yeah, what?" she said.

"What do you... ah, say, what do you call this?"

"I call it a bacon sandwich. What do you call it, fish and chips?" said the waitress, who didn't care for being shouted at.

Hiram raised his voice over the café's steamy coffee machine to about the level of a jumbo jet engine and said: "Then may ah POLITELY ask, where is the bacon?"

The waitress lifted a bit of bread. "There," she said, "it's the stuff between this bit of bread and this bit of bread."

She walked off to get his coffee.

I hope you haven't ordered a frothy coffee, thought Nat, *it might be a bit frothier than you would like.*

"One flob-accinno coming up," said Darius, guessing what Nat was thinking.

"In Texas, when we ask for a bacon sandwich we get half a pig between two loaves!" yelled Mr Wartburger III. Everyone in the cafe was now looking at them. Nat moved her chair away and looked at a picture on the wall, trying to pretend he was nothing to do with her.

"Everything's bigger in Texas," said Darius.

"That's right," said Hiram.

"Like the cars."

"Massive, yup."

"And houses."

"Huge, you got it."

"And people's heads."

"Definitely," said Hiram, "They're very big."

"And their mouths?"

"That's right, we got great big mouths, and they're bigger than anyone else's mouths, and don't you forget it, sonny boy."

By now the whole café was laughing.

Hiram stopped and frowned.

"Hey…" he said, glaring at Darius, but Darius had put on his best blank expression, the one Nat knew he used when he was pretending not to understand something in maths because he couldn't be bothered to do it.

And then… Hiram threw back his head and burst into the loudest – and most embarrassing

– laugh Nat had ever heard. "Ha ha ha. That's good, that's real good, you got me," he said crying tears of laughter and shaking his head.

Afterwards, they walked around town, with Tiffannee pointing out some of her favourite places; the cinema, the swimming baths, the nail bar. According to Hiram, everything was 'cute' and 'adorable' just like his 'hunny bunny'. Nat started feeling a bit sick.

So she wasn't keen when Hiram insisted on taking everyone to "one of those quaint old tea rooms" next because he'd heard so much about them.

"They're on every street corner in England, right?" said Hiram, over the noise of the traffic. "The ones with the thatched roofs, roses up the wall, little old ladies on bicycles with big pots of tea and muffins and cucumber sandwiches, am I right?"

Nat looked around at the street. There was a mini-mart and a tattoo parlour, a 24-hour locksmiths, a cab office and a charity shop.

"We might have to go into the countryside," said Dad, "for the whole thatched roof thing."

"OK, let's walk to the countryside. It can't be far, your whole island is tiny."

Even Tiffannee looked embarrassed now.

"Well, might be easier if we drive," said Dad, who liked to help. "Hop in the Atomic Dustbin, we'll find somewhere."

As Nat clambered in she hissed, "Just don't go anywhere that you might want to go to again, ever."

"Don't be like that," said Dad. "He'll be family in three weeks,"

Nat groaned. She hadn't thought it possible, but this wedding was getting WORSE by the second.

"How's the brilliant plan coming on?" she hissed at Darius. He rubbed his stomach, which was as tight as a drum.

"Too full too think," he burped, contentedly.

Yes, thought Nat, worse and worse.

CHAPTER SIX

. . . .

A LITTLE LATER AND THE SUN HAD COME OUT AND Dad had stumbled on a lovely tea room in the kind of perfect, rose-clad cottage that make Americans go weak at the knees.

"Lemme tell you about our vision for the wedding," said Hiram J Loudmouth, as they sat in the little garden at the back of DINGLEY DELL TEA ROOMS AND COUNTRY FAYRE SHOPPE. He munched on an enormous slice of Victoria sponge, scattering crumbs as he spoke.

"Magical, fairytale, ye olde worlde, English, retro, vintage, countryside, historical, garden," said Tiffannee, counting off the 'buzz words' on her fingers.

"It's modern, but with a traditional twist," agreed Hiram.

"Yes, yes, we know," said Nat, "we've been organising it for you for ages now."

"Yes, but I think we can do *more*," he said. "Since I've been here, I've been stuffing myself with your culture."

And cake, thought Nat, wiping crumbs off her top.

"You've got a church booked, you've got six Perfect Fairy Princesses…" began Dad.

"Five," corrected Tiffannee, "one *so-called friend* has let me down and won't even say why!"

That'll be hair and eyebrow-less Bella then, thought Nat.

"You know, Tiffannee cried for two solid hours when she found out," said Hiram. "The hurt that selfish woman has caused…"

"At least she wasn't family," breathed Tiffannee. "Can you imagine?"

I'm trying not to, thought Nat, wincing inwardly.

"…and then you're going to that posh castle golf club hotel where there's a lunch and then a band and a disco," said Dad, carrying on. "And wedding centrepieces," he added, quickly.

"OK so we got the *basics*," said Hiram, "but where's the maypole?"

Dunno where it is but I know where I'd like to put it, thought Nat.

"Erm…" said Dad.

"Maypole. We want old English, right? So we need morris dancers, a jack in the green, a troupe of mummers…"

"…some jugglers, clowns, folk singers, food vans, hog roast," Tiffannee finished.

"Let me write all this down," said Dad, confused. "Do you want these before or after the disco?"

An hour later Dad's notebook was full and he looked frazzled.

"We'll never get all this organised in time," Nat said to Darius, when the pair of them went inside to order more tea. Darius looked thoughtful.

"Keep agreeing to do everything she wants. You have to look like you really REALLY want to go," he said.

"It'll make your excuse later look way more believable."

"Yes, yes, but what's my excuse gonna *be*?"

"One thing at a time," said Darius, sticking his fingers in YE OLDE COUNTRY JAMME pots.

Nat had to listen to more wedding drivel all afternoon. She tried to look interested but probably failed. And then the loud American grabbed her and said: "You know, you're very important to Tiffannee, Nathalia!"

"Why's that?" said Nat.

"Tiffannee had a dream of six Fairy Princess Bridesmaids and you were chosen sixth. Which makes you top of the Fairy Princess Bridesmaid pyramid. The most important."

"Or it makes me the *last* princess chosen which makes me bottom of the fairy princess pile. The LEAST important," said Nat.

"Plus you're *family*," said Tiffannee, giving Nat a little squeeze, then smoothing out her dress. There it is again, thought Nat, that rotten word 'family.' Every time she tried to get out of anything recently, someone would say: 'it's for family', as if that explained everything. It was driving her bananas.

"In fact, I have an announcement to make. Now Bella has deserted me, I want you to be… Second Assistant Bridesmaid!" said Tiffannee, grandly.

"Yay," said Nat, not very grandly at all. She scowled at Darius.

"But we do have one teensy weensy problem,"

said Tiffannee, "and we need your help."

Nat was going to complain, but Darius nudged her and raised a crafty eyebrow.

Here goes with the evil plan, thought Nat. "OK," she said. "Of course I'll help. I'd *love* to help."

"Is it about the entertainment?" said Dad excitedly.

"No," said Hiram.

"I've had some genius ideas about that," said Dad.

"It's not about the entertainment," said Tiffannee.

"Let me just tell you anyway," burbled Dad.

Nat cringed. Dad was *always* keen to do the entertainment, anywhere and everywhere they went.

And it was always a total disaster. From school quiz nights ending in riots to birthday parties ending in casualty, from holidays that landed them in jail to discos that ended with her naked baby botty projected ten metres high, Dad was the WORST entertainer on the planet.

"Joke-a-oke!" said Dad. Everyone looked blank, "It's like karaoke, but people stand up and tell great jokes from a screen, rather than sing rubbish songs."

"Whose jokes?" said Tiffannee.

"My jokes," said Dad.

"No," said Hiram, Tiffannee and Nat together.

"OK, then how about I get my old college band back together, just for your wedding?" said Dad, hopefully. "King Ivor and the Hunnypots — we could do a great set for you, no problem."

"Dad, no one liked your band when you were young and thin and had hair," said Nat.

Dad just laughed.

"He can't resist it," said Nat, annoyed, "he'll do anything to get attention, he's worse than a bride." She looked at Tiffannee. "No offence," she added, quickly.

Darius said nothing, but Nat noticed he was

looking at Dad with the weird expression that she knew meant he'd had an idea or else was about to armpit fart the national anthem.

"Back to me, people," said Tiffannee, "you know, the bride?"

"We're all ears," said Dad.

Tiffannee looked pained. "It's Uncle Ernie," she said, "I think I've made a terrible mistake."

"Did you forget to invite him?" said Dad, "because it's OK, he's quite a distant relative, he won't mind."

"No, I did invite him, that's the problem," said Tiffannee, awkwardly.

Even super-confident Hiram looked uncomfortable. "It was MY fault," he said, "I wanted Tiff to have the biggest and best wedding ever so I invited everyone she knew... without asking her."

"Including Uncle Ernie," said Tiffannee.

"What's the problem?" said Nat. She thought Tiffannee looked embarrassed. *That's odd,* she thought, *it's usually me looking embarrassed.*

"She wants a PERFECT wedding, not the biggest," said Hiram, "and she doesn't think uncle Ernie is, well, the perfect guest."

"He's a long way from perfect," said Tiffannee, though flushing red and looking a bit uncomfortable for saying it.

Nat was so shocked she couldn't speak. She thought everyone in her family was used to having embarrassing relatives.

"Uncle Ernie is so weird-looking he'll ruin the photos," said Tiffannee, squirming a little, "and so full of wind he'll ruin the magic and romance of the ceremony with trumpet noises and the smell of rotten eggs."

"So?" said Nat.

Tiffannee's eyes filled with tears. "So Daddy promised me a perfect wedding but he can't be here right now to make it perfect. He's still stuck in Texas because there's this teeny-tiny oil spill and they're saying it's his fault."

"An oil spill? Who put someone from Dad's family in charge of an oil well?" said Nat, "you can't trust a Bumolé with a wedding."

The other customers in the tea room stopped chewing and started listening.

Nat cringed; she hated her embarrassing family surname – and all the terrible nicknames it had earned her – and hadn't meant to say it out loud. But she carried on anyway.

"Dad can't even be trusted with a tin opener. And on that note, have you seen him with a glue gun? Last time he tried to make a model aeroplane he glued a German dive-bomber to his nose and went to casualty."

Dad chuckled. Nat glared at him.

"And you put the plane stickers all over your face. You had swastikas all over your forehead and no-one in the hospital would talk to you. Except that one man and he had some very odd ideas."

Tiffannee's lip wobbled. "At least your dad's

here," she sobbed. "And your dad would make YOUR wedding day perfect."

I doubt that very much indeed, thought Nat.

Hiram hugged Tiffannee, and Dad put an arm around her too.

"Watch the dress," she sniffed, "it's di Milano."

"Sorry," said Dad, taking his arm away.

"And you're the closest thing to my dad I've got," wailed Tiffannee, "which means you're supposed to be my dad until my dad gets here."

Dad couldn't bear the sight of a crying woman. "What can I do?" he said, "you can't un-invite Uncle Ernie, there's a small chance you might look like a terrible person if you do."

"I know," she said, "that's why *she's* got to do it for me." Tiffannee turned to Nat. "You're so sweet and clever, you can let him down gently, I'm too upset to talk to him. And you're my second assistant chief bridesmaid. AND you said you'd help."

Nat's mouth was open in disbelief. She

looked at Darius, who had told her to agree to everything the bride wanted. He gave her a quick thumbs-up.

You'd better have a good plan brewing, she thought.

"I'd be very glad to help," she heard herself say, "anything for you."

"You're a darling," said Tiffannee, "thank you."

"That's settled then," said Hiram. "Sorry y'all but you gotta fire 'im."

CHAPTER SEVEN

. . . .

"I CAN'T BELIEVE I'M DOING THIS," COMPLAINED Nat, standing outside Uncle Ernie's front door later that afternoon. She looked around at his neat and tidy front garden, full of novelty gnomes, and wished she was somewhere else. "Uncle Ernie's really nice. Everyone likes him. This is going to be horrible."

But Darius had said she had to play along with Tiffannee's wedding plans, even the barmy ones.

"He likes you," said Dad. "You can help let him down gently."

Dad rang the doorbell. Instead of a *bong*, it sang a happy little tune.

"*Hello guests, you are welcome, hello guests,*" trilled the doorbell, before what sounded like a choir of gnomes chimed in:

"*HELLOOOOO GUESTS!*"

"Coming!" shouted Uncle Ernie from inside. "I'm just painting Tiffannee and Hiram and my hands are sticky."

"Are all our relatives a bit loopy, Dad?" asked Nat.

"Only on your nan's side," said Dad. After a minute the door opened and Uncle Ernie was standing there with a big beaming smile which very nearly covered his unusual face. It was round and jolly, like the moon. And like the moon, it was also grey and warty, like it had been battered by meteorites.

Lovely Uncle Ernie opened the door and gave Nat and Dad a huge welcoming hug before leading them in. There was a smell of fresh paint, and rotten eggs. Uncle Ernie burbled away, unaware of the doom hurtling towards him.

"Tea and cakes for everyone!" said Uncle Ernie. "Make yourself at home, my home is your home, as you know, I'll just pop the kettle on."

"Can't stop long," said Dad, "we just dropped by with some wedding news."

"Dad – shush and look," whispered Nat, tugging at his sleeve.

"Not now, I've got myself ready to drop the bombshell," said Dad.

There was a ripping noise from the kitchen.

"Sorry, sprout and baked bean soup," shouted Ernie, "I like to experiment."

"I think Ernie's dropping his own bombshells," Dad went on, but Nat was too worried to find it funny, and she couldn't tear her eyes away from…

Dad raised his voice. "I reckon you'll probably think this is good news, it'll save you a lot of bother and free up a weekend for some fun. On balance. I think you'll be relieved."

"DAD!" insisted Nat. "Shuddup and look at that."

She was pointing at something in the middle of the living room. Standing proud were two freshly painted, enormous, *bride and groom* gnomes!

"Oooh, do you like them?" said Uncle Ernie, returning and pointing at his wedding masterpiece. "They're for Tiffannee and Hiram's wedding."

"I'd never have guessed," said Nat. "I mean, you wouldn't HAVE to give them to her for the wedding, there's plenty of other uses for them, like, er, um, lemmee think…"

"I made them myself out of matchsticks. There's four hundred hours of work in each of them, but it was worth it."

"Was it though?" said Nat, wondering how to let him down gently. "Was it really worth it?"

"Oh yes," said Uncle Ernie, coughing as

another little explosion popped out behind him. "I know I'm only a distant relative, but I do remember lovely, sweet little Rosie – I mean Tiffannee now isn't it – before she went abroad. She was so kind and gentle."

"People change," said Nat. "They can change a lot, actually."

Uncle Ernie dabbed a tear from his eye. "This wedding has made me feel an important part of the family. Especially as I never had kids of my own, and since my wife left me for the window cleaner I've been so lonely."

"I thought your windows were looking a bit dirty," said Dad. Nat kicked him. Hard.

"I told you I wasn't very good at this," whispered Dad, as Uncle Ernie went back into the kitchen to pour the tea. "You say something to him."

"Are you nuts?" hissed Nat. "He's made WEDDING GNOMES. Enormous, horrible, four-hundred-hour wedding gnomes."

"He'd probably have made those anyway," said Dad. "He likes gnomes."

"Shut up, Dad. Oh we *can't* un-invite him just because he won't look good in the stupid wedding pictures and he pongs like a rubbish dump in a heatwave. It's horrid."

"You'd better think of something else then," said Dad wandering off to the loo, "he's coming back."

But Nat couldn't think of anything and she spent the next few minutes getting more and more uncomfortable as Uncle Ernie burbled on about how much he was looking forward to the wedding.

Finally, Nat couldn't stand it any longer. She had to go for it. She cleared her throat. "Thing is, Uncle Ernie…" she began, but never got to finish her sentence because just then a huge shaggy-haired dog bounded into the room and leapt on Uncle Ernie, almost completely smothering him. Uncle Ernie laughed and tickled the hound, who rolled on its back happily, pink tongue lolling out.

"Hello, Buster, were you asleep, boy?" said Uncle Ernie, now covered in dog hair. "Yes you were, yes you were!"

The dog woofed happily. "This is my new dog," he said to Nat, "Buster. He's a rescue mutt. They said at the pound that he's got no sense of smell. Can you imagine how terrible that must be for a dog?"

A sprout-and-baked-bean-flavoured rumble wobbled the sofa.

"It might not be so bad," said Nat, through watery eyes.

"He's my bestest friend in the whole world now," cooed uncle Ernie. "I never leave the house without him, not even for ten minutes."

A small ray of hope filled Nat's feverish brain.

"No dogs at the wedding," she blurted out. "Tiffannee is very very allergic. She could swell up and die."

"Oh no, that's terrible for the poor girl!" said Uncle Ernie, trumping in sympathy. "I can't imagine life without a doggie."

"She's very upset about it," fibbed Nat, "poor poor Tiffannee. Poor lovely, upset, *sweet, kind, wonderful* Tiffannee."

"I can't abandon Buster though," said Uncle Ernie, looking at Nat, damp-eyed at the thought of it. "He's been abandoned before."

"Oh dear dear dear," said Nat, "what will you do?"

Uncle Ernie sighed. "It is with a heavy heart and much regret that I will have to forego the pleasure of the nuptuals."

"Just to be clear – that does mean you're not going, right?" said Nat.

"Don't see how I can. I'll write my apologies tonight. Still, how lovely to be asked."

Inside, Nat jumped for joy! But then...

Dad came in, mouthing: *Have you told him?* at Nat. She smiled what she hoped was a sad smile.

"Dad, Uncle Ernie's not coming to the wedding, sadly."

"Oh, well done, Nat," said Dad, relieved. "I knew you could do it." He patted Uncle Ernie on the shoulder. "Sorry, fancy Tiffannee saying you can't come just because you won't look good in the photos. I mean, who looks good in photos? I know I don't. And as to trouser trumpets, well, she could buy a clothes peg for her nose, couldn't she?"

Nat looked at her dad in horror. There was a horrible *horrible* silence.

Thirty seconds later, Dad and Nat were driving away at high speed to the sound of gnomes being smashed back to matchsticks.

CHAPTER EIGHT

. . . .

"DID YOU DO WHAT YOUR COUSIN WANTED?" said Darius at school on Monday. Nat was visiting him in the corridor outside the Head's office, where he'd been sent for writing an essay called:

What were the causes of my bum ache?

Instead of:

What were the causes of the first world war?

His excuse that he 'must have heard it wrong' didn't get him out of the punishment.

"Yes, I did it, and it was *horrible*," said Nat, shuddering at the memory. "There was a massive family row about upsetting Uncle Ernie.

"I said I didn't deserve to be a bridesmaid because I'd done the deed, which was pretty clever of me. But then stupid dad stood up for me and so I'm still a flipping fairy."

Darius didn't say anything. He seemed to be deep in thought. He was supposed to be writing "I must not be so very very rude" out a hundred times but instead Nat saw he was working on verse 541 of his epic poem 'diarrhoea'.

"Your plan isn't working, is what I'm saying," said Nat getting impatient. "I'm still a flipping bridesmaid, in fact now I'm Second Assistant Bridesmaid, and now even more people hate me, not just the other bridesmaids. Do you have a plan yet?"

"Interesting. If everyone hated you, they wouldn't want you around, would they?" said Darius. Nat looked at the empty corridor. She guessed Darius must know how that felt.

"Yeah, but Tiffannee doesn't hate me – she just promoted me. In *her* eyes I'm a hero because I broke the bad news to Ernie. On top of that she's taking me and the other bridesmaids to the funfair on Saturday. Says she's heard a rumour that things haven't been PERFECT between us bridesmaids so we need to do some bridesmaid bonding."

"Invite me," said Darius.

"You said that last time, and look what happened," said Nat. "You're supposed to be conjuring up an evil plan, not having a fun time at the funfair," snapped Nat.

"Just do it," he said. He went back to his poem. "Oh, and can you think of a rhyme for 'splatter'?"

Darius and Nat met Tiffannee near the entrance to the busy funfair the following weekend.

Tiffannee had obviously spent AGES in the

beauty salon because it was like looking at a shop window dummy. She had PERFECT skin, with blindingly white teeth and white-blonde hair that didn't move.

In fact, nothing much on Tiffannee's face moved, even when she talked.

"Every time I see her, she looks more perfect and less pretty," Nat said to Daruis, who just belched, loudly.

"I'm not sure your choice of breakfast was entirely wise," said Nat, taking a step away from him. "Cream soda, boiled sweets, mints and chocolate aren't really any of your five a day."

"No kisses, you'll spoil my make-up!" said Tiffannee, waving Nat away. She smoothed the creases from her smart, bright-white dress.

"Oh heavens, it's little Darius," said Tiffannee, jumping back several feet as the terror of 8H trundled into view.

Nat had to admit that her friend was looking even more rank than usual.

Tiffannee looked like an angel, Darius looked like something from the other end of the afterlife.

Tiffannee tore her gaze away from the tiny monster, who was now stuffing a huge puffball of pink candyfloss into his mouth, and grabbed Nat. "Thank you for being such a fab bridesmaid," she said. "Bella walking out like that after the spa was a total let down, but at least I know after what you did for me with Uncle Ernie I can rely on you. You're *family*."

Nat looked at Darius and shuffled her feet uncomfortably. A few metres away, the other bridesmaids were gossiping in a huddle. They were next to a large, brightly painted old-fashioned merry-go-round. They all glared at Nat, jealously.

"Don't mention it," Nat stammered, looking nervously at the other bridesmaids. "I mean, really, please don't keep mentioning it."

"This won't do, this won't do, you're all wrong, I can't work with this!" screeched a woman with a severe short haircut wearing combat trousers, army boots and a black leather jacket. She seemed to be shouting at the bridesmaids, who were now backing away from her in terror.

"That's Clara Bunion, my official wedding photographer," said Tiffannee proudly. "She's come here to get to know us all. She normally does wars and stuff, but my dad persuaded her to come and do my wedding."

"Wars?" said Nat.

"Yes, between me and you, she's been suffering from stress a bit so she thought this might be a nice break for her. Just don't make any loud bangs or come up behind her suddenly, she's still a bit jumpy. She's only just back from the front line."

Is everyone in the entire world raving bonkers except me? wondered Nat.

"Listen to Clara everyone!" shouted Tiffannee turning to the bridesmaids. "She's a VERY talented photographer. Do as you're told and nobody gets hurt. Hahaha, just my little joke there."

Clara smiled a tight, firm smile. She drew herself up to her full height and addressed the bride and bridesmaids like a general addressing her troops.

"Now, we want to make these pictures look as natural as possible, so you must do EXACTLY as you're told."

"Where's your camera?" asked Nat, who was quite interested in taking pictures. She had taken some great selfies, just with her phone, and she fancied getting her hands on a big proper camera.

"Photographs are not about pictures. Photographs are about LIFE," said Clara, snorting like a horse.

"Photographs are A BIT about pictures too, though, aren't they?" said Nat, confused.

"You are a child, you don't understand," said Clara. Tiffannee and the bridesmaids all giggled. Nat felt foolish.

"Clara is saying she needs to *live* with us before she takes pictures," said Tiffannee. "Anyone can take pictures; Clara makes ART."

"How long is she going to live with us?" said Nat, worried. "Only I don't think there's much in for tea."

Tiffannee laughed again. "Clara only needs to be with us for a few hours to understand who we are. Artists live differently to us; they see the world more clearly."

"I can see Tiffannee has a pure, white soul," said Clara, "which is why today I have dressed her in pure white."

Nat looked at herself. She was in jeans and a plain grey T-shirt. She felt drab and dull and boring compared to Tiffannee. "Should I get changed?" Nat said. Clara looked her up and down.

"No," she said, "drab suits you."

Oh thanks, thought Nat.

"Shouldn't we be in our bridesmaid outfits?"

asked suck-up Chief Bridesmaid Daisy Wetwipe.

Nat went cold. *Noooo*, she thought. *Not the Esmerelda. Not in PUBLIC.*

But Clara shook her head violently.

"This is very simple, so I will only say it once. There is a wedding *story* here, understand? You will NOT be fairy princesses until the wedding day, when your queen –" she pointed at Tiffannee – "is crowned. Until then, think of yourselves as caterpillars, before you can become the butterfly."

"Isn't she the best?" said Tiffannee. "She knows that a wedding is a story. A story about love. Perfect, perfect love."

The bridesmaids all clapped and smiled, apart from Nat, who felt a bit queasy, like she'd eaten too much sugar off a spoon made of honey.

They watched as Clara started posing Tiffannee and the other bridesmaids, hopping up and then crouching down, with her hands in front of her face, as if she was taking photos.

"I don't think that madwoman even *has* a camera," muttered Darius.

"The sun's all wrong!" shouted Clara. "No pictures this morning, so we just have to BE."

She grabbed Nat and pushed her into the bridesmaids. "Be what?" said Nat, confused.

Clara snorted again.

I'm gonna get you a bale of hay and a saddle soon, thought Nat.

"She means we have to just go on the rides and behave like any normal bridesmaids having a wonderful day out with the amazing, beautiful bride," said Tilly Saddle.

Tiffannee clapped her hands with glee. Tilly simpered.

What a crawly bumlick you are, thought Nat.

"Follow me!" cried the war journalist, marching off into the funfair. The others began trooping after her. Darius, who had just grabbed a hot dog, tagged along behind them.

Chief Bridesmaid and chief horrible girl Daisy

Wetwipe suddenly stopped and pointed at him. He had tomato sauce smeared over his face and bits of onion down his chin.

"He can't come, can he?" said Daisy.

Oooh you are mean, thought Nat, then felt guilty because she often felt exactly the same.

Clara advanced on Darius. He swallowed the last of his hot dog and burped noisily.

"No, the little hobgoblin MUST come," she said, unexpectedly. She grabbed him, then immediately let go and wiped her hands down her trousers.

"Can't you see the contrast between you – the beautiful fairy princesses – and this... this *thing*?"

"So having him in the background makes us look even more gorgeous!" squealed Daisy.

"That's a brilliant idea," said Tiffannee.

"Yes, because I am brilliant," said Clara. "Now stop talking, I'm the only person to talk from now on, understood? TO THE DODGEMS!"

CHAPTER NINE

. . . .

THE BRIDESMAIDS AND THE GOBLIN SPENT THE next noisy, dizzying hour on the rides. Nat even enjoyed herself a little, although she was cross with Darius for not having a plan, and just getting a free day out at the fair.

He was behaving very oddly. Every time they changed rides, he dashed to a fast-food stall, or a sweetie van.

"How can you eat all that rubbish before going on a ride?" said Nat. "The rides make my stomach churn as it is."

Darius didn't reply; he was too busy stuffing his face with a bag of extra-sweet chocolate fudge brownies.

Clara still refused to take pictures, saying she wanted to capture what was REAL, and the bridesmaids weren't being real enough. Even the bride-to-be was flagging now.

"Oh, how can you say that?" moaned Tiffannee after the fifth ride. "We're as real as can be."

She gave her best fake smile. So did the other bridesmaids.

But it was no use. "When you have looked, as I have, into the face of horror," said Clara, "you know what is real. Those are the only pictures I take."

She pointed to the biggest, baddest ride in the park:

THE DESTRUCTORATER.

It looked like the inside of a dinosaur skeleton. It glinted and gleamed and stood taller than the sky.

NO ONE who was sane wanted to go on it.

"Me first," said Darius, grabbing Nat's hand and dragging her with him.

"Follow the goblin, bridesmaids," ordered Clara.

The others nervously obeyed. Soon they were all strapped in their carriage, Darius and Nat in the front seat, Clara just behind them, and the rest of the bridal party in the back. Nat started moaning that she didn't fancy this ride, but Darius wasn't listening – he was forcing down a huge, meaty Cornish pasty, full of chunks of beef and veg.

The carriage lurched forward and Darius burped the National Anthem.

The rollercoaster was horrible. It looped and twisted and rolled and went backwards and just when everyone thought with relief it was over, it started doing it all over again.

Nat thought her eyes were going to pop out.

She felt dizzy and sick and was very glad she hadn't spent all morning eating rubbishy junk food. Like Darius.

She looked at him. He was very pale and trembly. Little beads of sweat were popping out on his forehead.

"You all right?" she said, anxiously. Darius just grinned an evil grin. Nat recognised this grin as a signal.

A signal to be very afraid.

Tiffannee and the bridesmaids, strapped in behind them, were pretending to enjoy the ride, but now they just had that grim look on their faces worn by parents taking their eight-year-old daughters to a boy band concert.

They were at the top of the biggest dip, just about to hurtle to the ground. Everyone looked terrified.

"I am ready to make the pictures!" yelled Clara, mad hair flailing. She produced a big camera from an inexplicable hiding place. "THIS is real life. I need real, and now I have real."

The carriage shot forward.

"Duck," said dizzy Darius, whose eyes were spinning. His face was literally green.

Nat immediately ducked, so missed seeing what happened next.

What happened next was THE MOST DISGUSTING THING that Darius had ever done. You have been warned.

BLEUUURGH! went Darius.

And launched his lunch.

WHEEE! flew the contents of his over-stretched stomach – half-digested candy-floss, hot dogs (including ketchup and onions), chomped donuts, slimy fudge and lots of bits of sticky peanut brittle.

The pitter-pattering peanuts were the worst.

Or maybe the meaty chunks from the pasty.

AAAAARHH! screamed the bridesmaids as the vile pile of vom hurtled through the air.

Right at them.

SPLATTT!

"BRILLIANT expressions!" yelled the bonkers snapper, taking photos like mad. "Now I am getting real. I am looking into your souls."

"Stop taking pictures!" screamed a sick-splattered Tiffannee over the sound of all her bridesmaids shrieking and weeping and wailing.

"The horror, the horror!" yelled the photographer with wild glee.

"You're sacked, Clara!" shouted Tiffannee.

"What's happening?" said Nat, who had her head buried under her arms for safety. The rollercoaster swooped down to the ground and stopped.

"That's better," said Darius, hopping out, wiping his mouth on his sleeve. "Fancy a burger?"

"SHE'S DONE IT ON PURPOSE!" screamed Daisy Wetwipe, who, by the look of it, had taken a direct hit. "She's teamed up with the goblin from hell to get rid of us. She wants to be Chief Fairy Princess Bridesmaid and she won't stop until she is!"

"Yes, you HAVE to stop her coming to the wedding," said Tilly, who was almost as decorated.

"Sack her too, sack her *right now*," demanded Erin Granule.

"She'll stop at nothing, I tell you," said Annie Chicken, "NOTHING."

"Is this true, Nathalia?" said Tiffannee. "Are you really so desperate to be my Chief Bridesmaid that you're trying to nobble the others?"

Nat was outraged. She was about to furiously deny it all when SHE REALISED THE PLAN!

She could have hugged Darius, except he'd gone to the loos to sponge down.

This was her big chance to get out of Tiffannee's wedding! It was so easy.

"Yes, I admit it," she said, holding her hands up. "I'm guilty as charged."

She thought she might as well do her confession

properly and decided to give it a touch of the Juliets. They'd been doing that rubbish play at school and she thought it was pretty feeble stuff, but she did like the sound of the words.

"By my truth, I swear being a Perfect Fairy Princess Bridesmaid has been my greatest dream ever since I was a child, and I could not rest until my Fairy Princess rivals were all defeated. But in my defence, it's only because I love you with my heart, goodly cousin. Now punish me. I think banishment should do it."

But to her great dismay, tears welled up in Tiffannee's eyes. She opened her vom-splattered arms and grabbed Nat.

There was a squishing noise.

Don't hug me, don't hug me, ew ew ew, thought Nat, followed by: *I* might *have overdone the speech a bit.*

"I forgive you," said Tiffannee.

"Don't forgive me," said Nat, "I'm unforgivable."

"It's only because you care so much."

"And because I'm a wicked wicked person who definitely needs to be taught the error of her wicked flipping ways."

Tiffannee turned to the miserable bridesmaids. "This little girl is the best bridesmaid EVER," said Tiffannee. "And what's more, she's my *family*. Anyone who disagrees can get lost."

There was a pause. Eventually, Erin Granule stormed off saying, "I'm not sticking around, who knows what she'll do next."

"Anybody else feel like that?" said Tiffannee, putting an arm around Nat.

Me! thought Nat, *I feel like that!*

No one else moved.

"Meet my new First Assistant Chief Bridesmaid," said Tiffannee.

Nat looked round. Then she realised…

Tiffannee meant HER.

CHAPTER TEN

· · · ·

ON MONDAY AT SCHOOL NAT WASN'T TALKING TO Darius. Except to shout at him.

"You've just made it worse," she said. "Your plans are rubbish. I keep getting promoted. At this rate I'll end up being the bride."

"There's one more plan," he said. "I was saving it for emergencies."

"This is an emergency."

"It's risky," said Darius, "it's very risky."

"I DON'T CARE," said Nat, "will it get me out of fairy princess horror?"

Darius paused. "No, it's too risky," he said eventually.

"Darius Bagley, if you don't tell me, I'm gonna tell everyone you want to kiss Penny Posnitch."

"Fine," said Darius, "get your dad to come in to my house when you drop me off after school, and just play along. No time to explain."

Last lesson of the day was maths and Nat always sat next to Darius because he told her the answers but however hard she poked him and scowled at him, he wouldn't tell her his brilliant plan.

She was wracking her brains about it, when Mr Frantz the permanently harassed maths teacher passed her desk. Normally when he looked at her, she was staring out of the window with an utterly blank expression.

"Vot are you concentrating so hard on?" he said suspiciously. "You are girl with maths brain of wombat."

"Maths things, sir," she said. "Numbers,

mainly. Really big numbers."

Darius, sitting next to her, blew snot bubbles out of his nose and Mr Frantz suddenly remembered why he never usually stood near these two children.

At last the bell for the end of class went and Nat shoved Darius rudely towards the door, hoping to get out of the school gates and up the road before Dad could pull up in the Atomic Dustbin and embarrass her, but as they approached the gates she realised it was too late.

PAAAAARP!

The farty car horn blared out and literally everyone at the gates turned round. Nat felt her face going red, knowing immediately what vehicle was making the horrible noise even before she heard Dad's cheery call: "Nat, over here, Nat! Stop pretending you can't see me! Stop turning around and walking the other way. Quick, you're going to have to jump in while we're still moving. I've opened the big slidey door so it's easy... Hurry up, I can't actually stop or the engine cuts out for various mechanical reasons I don't quite understand yet," yelled Dad. "Get a move on, I've driven past the school gates three times already and I think the school bus drivers are now trying to kill me."

Nat put her head down in the vain hope no one could see her and ran for the horrible, smoky old van, Darius trailing behind.

As soon as they got in, Darius immediately started to wrestle with the dog, trying to get his dog biscuit off him. The pair thrashed around on the floor in the back of the van until they eventually pulled up outside Darius's scruffy little house in the litter-strewn street.

There was a police car sitting outside. "Oh dear," said Dad. "Darius, I think Oswald might be in trouble again."

"Nah, it's just Fiona," said Darius, "Oswald's fiancée."

"Fiancée?" said Dad and Nat in unison.

Dad was stunned; Nat was FUMING; why hadn't Darius told her?

"Yes, they're getting married," said Darius hopping out of the van.

"Married?" repeated Dad. "Oswald's getting married? Oswald, your *brother* Oswald? Oswald Bagley's getting married?" Nat couldn't believe the news. Oswald Bagley, who looked after Darius since neither of his parents were around, was probably the hairiest and most terrifying man since the Viking Lord, Olaf the Hairy and Terrifying, who could scare people to death by smiling at them. Nat had never seen Oswald smile; she didn't think he could.

"Just WHO is mad enough to marry your brother?" asked Nat.

"It's a policewoman," said Darius. "She said it was easier to marry him than keep arresting him. Come in and meet her."

He hopped out of the van and scampered towards the door chewing half a soggy dog biscuit. Nat stomped furiously after him while Dad locked the van.

"And when exactly were you going to tell me about this?" fumed Nat.

"When it was important," said Darius simply. "And now it's important."

She stormed after her friend up the untidy garden path to the battered, weather-peeled front door. The front door wasn't locked – even in this part of town no one was mad enough to try and pinch anything from Oswald Bagley – so Darius pushed it with his foot and sauntered on in.

Nat couldn't believe what she saw. The front room was usually littered with half-drunk bottles, and almost empty of furniture, with old upturned beer crates for seats. There were generally missing floorboards and a wide and interesting selection of other people's belongings lying around.

But not today. Today the room had a carpet, a small table and a proper little sofa. The windows were clean, most of the smell had gone, and there was even a little vase of garden flowers on the windowsill.

"Wrong house," said Nat, turning to go back out.

A second later, Nat heard a woman's pretty voice singing a song and a second after that, Oswald Bagley's bride-to-be walked in from the kitchen, carrying a tray of tea and slices of cake.

"*Definitely* wrong house," said Nat, but Darius grabbed her arm and led her further into the front room, swiping a bit of cake on the way past and chucking himself down on the sofa.

"Shoes off," said the woman, with a firmer edge to her voice than the singing voice would suggest. She turned to Nat. She wasn't tall, but there was a solidness to her, like the stump of a tree. Her face was rather round and her hair rather short. She had fierce, intelligent blue eyes and very white teeth. She was also wearing a police uniform.

"You must be the famous Buttface," said the woman smiling.

"Must I?" said Nat, glaring at Darius, who grinned. The woman shot a sharp glance at him. "Sorry, Darius said you liked your nickname. I can see he's been rather naughty again, bless him. Sit down, have a cup of tea."

Nat sat next to Darius as the woman bustled around her. "Now, what should I call you?" she asked. "I'm Fiona. Fiona Sweetly. Police Constable Fiona Sweetly, in actual fact. I can't stay long, I'm actually on duty, but if Oswald doesn't get his afternoon cuppa he gets a bit cranky."

"Is he here?" said Nat, not wanting to think about a cranky Oswald.

"He's in the garden, doing something with the hollyhocks."

"Fire-bombing them?" joked Nat. Well, *half*-joked. Fiona's face grew stern, then softened. "I suppose I must accept Oswald has a bit of a reputation," said his intended with a sigh, "but all that's going to change."

"Congratulations on your wedding," said Nat, shooting daggers at Darius again.

In response, Darius did something extraordinary. He rearranged his normally lumpen, blank-looking face into something similar to a normal twelve-year-old's.

"I told her about the wedding because we're such good friends," said Darius, grabbing Nat by the hand. Nat froze in shock. "We're almost family and that's what weddings are all about, right?"

Nat was going to say something but Darius quickly shoved another piece of cake in her mouth. She went red and her eyes bulged.

"We do everything together. I can't imagine not inviting her to anything that we do."

"Oh in that case, I'm sure we all feel the same about Buttf— I mean Nathalia," said PC Fiona Sweetly. "You MUST come to our wedding."

"That's unexpected," said Darius.

Nat looked at him closely. He was definitely up to something. But what?

"We've set a date and everything," said Fiona, "the last Saturday of the month."

Nat's heart somersaulted. THAT WAS THE SAME AS Tiffannee'S WEDDING. She realised what Darius was up to! She would have hugged him, if he wasn't so utterly revolting.

"That's if we can ever have one," said Fiona, angrily. "No one will give us a venue for the party, so it looks like the wedding will have to be postponed."

Oh no, thought Nat.

Just then, Dad came in. "Hello everyone, I—" Dad looked around at the tidy room. "Sorry, wrong house," he said, making to go out again.

"No, right house, Dad," said Nat, "and look, this is Fiona. Oswald's fiancée."

"Um, congratulations?" said Dad.

"And I'm very much invited to the wedding," said Nat, quickly, "and I have to go. Can't say no to a bride and I've said yes. I'm definitely going to her wedding."

"Oh, well that's very, ah, nice," fibbed Dad, "very nice indeed. Weddings, love 'em. Can't get enough of them, I say!"

"Oswald's in the back garden. You should go and say congratulations to him too," said Nat.

"Hmmm, I suppose so," said Dad, nervously, heading out there. As soon as he'd gone, Nat smiled her nicest smile at Fiona.

Fiona carried on. "Yes, it's terrible. We'd set the date for the end of the month, and sent out all the invitations and everything, but we can't find anywhere to have the party. Everywhere I try says they're full for the next five years. Even the big hotel in town said they weren't taking bookings until next century."

"Oh," said Nat, "you didn't tell them you were marrying Oswald, did you?"

"Of course I did," snapped Fiona. "Why?"

"No reason," said Nat and they sat in polite

silence until Dad came back.

When Fiona told Dad that they couldn't find anywhere to have the wedding reception, he said:

"You didn't tell them you were marrying Oswald, did you?"

"YES, of course I did!" snapped Fiona, even more snappily. "Why shouldn't I?"

"Well, that's your problem right there," said Dad cheerfully. "No one wants a Bagley wedding party under their roof. Can you imagine?"

Nat winced. Fiona grew even crosser.

"What's wrong with a Bagley wedding?" she said.

"There's nothing wrong with the wedding bit," said Dad. "It's more the massive drunken riot *after* the wedding that people get upset by."

Fiona sighed. "He really does have a teensy bit of a bad reputation, doesn't he? I hadn't thought of that. All of us down the police station love a Bagley wedding. We all get overtime and danger money. I'm actually paying for our honeymoon with the money I earned after the last Bagley wedding."

"That's quite romantic," said Dad, "in a weird way."

"Yes, but what are we going to do?" wailed Fiona. "We're running out of time. We need to get married on that very day."

"I couldn't agree more," said Nat.

"I went to see Merlin and he was quite sure of it. He said the giblets were very clear."

"Merlin?" said Dad.

"Giblets?" said Darius.

"Absolutely," said Nat.

"Merlin Tolpuddle is our New-Age astrologer and shaman. You might know him as a white witch," said Fiona.

"Or you might know him as the bloke who runs the dry-cleaner's," said Darius, quietly.

"He reads giblets, the way some of the lesser wizards read tea leaves," said Fiona. "Merlin swears by giblets; says you get a much clearer reading."

A bit of hedge sailed in through the back door.

Literally everyone in my life is stark raving mad, thought Nat, picking twigs out of her hair.

"Merlin's very kindly agreed to marry us," said Fiona.

"Is he a vicar?" said Nat.

"Oh, don't be so 20th century," said Fiona. "Lots of people can marry you these days. He got a special certificate to do it."

"From Gandalf," sniggered Darius.

Fiona scowled at him. "*Actually* he got it online, which just shows that you can be New Age AND new technology at the same time," she said, "so there."

"Nat's Dad's brilliant at organising weddings," said Darius innocently. "You should see the amazing one he's doing for Nat's cousin. It's ace. He's great."

If Fiona had known Darius better, she might have become suspicious at this point. But she didn't, and so she wasn't.

Nat knew Darius, and she realised what he was up to. He was tempting Dad…

"You definitely should get him to help, especially with the entertainment," added Darius. "He's awesome at that."

Nat knew Dad was RUBBISH at that.

But she knew – and crafty Darius knew – that Dad thought he was BRILLIANT at it.

"He's got this great idea for a new party game, called joke-a-oke," said Darius, "and he's in this fantastic band. What a shame you can't find somewhere to have your wedding."

"Can't you? Oh, I'm sure I could find you somewhere to have your party," said Dad, "and I'd happily do the entertainment too," he added. "All part of the service!"

Darius looked at Nat. He sat back, as if to say: mission accomplished, I am lord of all the evil plans.

Dad looked at Nat. He sat back, as if to say: I am lord of all wedding entertainment.

"Oh wow, that would be fantastic!" said Fiona. "Thank you so much."

"My pleasure," said Dad. "I'm a bit of a wedding guru these days."

"Would you really help us?" said Darius, laying it on a bit thick.

"Of course, Darius. First, I'll find you a place to have your wedding party. Then I'll throw you the best party this town's ever seen!"

Nat cringed. Still, even being forced to endure dad's terrible entertainment ideas was better than being a Perfect First Assistant Fairy Princess Bridesmaid. She could always hide from the former no such luck with the latter...

"You're amazing!" said Fiona, running over and hugging dad so hard his eyes bulged. She ran out to tell Oswald and came back with a chainsawed bunch of flowers. She handed them to Dad.

"It's his way of saying thanks," she said.

"So – when do you want the wedding?"

Fiona told him.

"That date rings a bell," said Dad. Then Nat watched as he realised... it was the same date as Tiffannee's!

Dad went very pale indeed.

Darius grinned an evil grin at Nat, who watched excitedly to see what Dad would do.

"Oh dear," said Dad, "now I hope you don't think I'm going to let you down, but—"

Fiona interrupted: "As do I," she said, in a steely way. "Oswald hates being let down. He really HATES it."

There was a massive roar as the chainsaw went into action again.

Dad sat back as if to say: I am Lord of Totally Doomed.

CHAPTER ELEVEN

· · · ·

"THAT WAS ROTTEN LUCK," SAID DAD, LOOKING pale as they drove away. "What are the chances? Two weddings, at the very same time!"

"I know, Dad, and I'm really upset," said Nat, trying desperately to stop giggling. "Obviously I have to go to Oswald's, but I ever so much wanted to be a Fairy Princess Bridesmaid. What a shame. What a terrible crying shame."

Her toes were literally wiggling with naughty pleasure inside her trainers.

"Really?" Dad looked at her suspiciously.

"You sure your pants aren't on fire?"

"Nope, quite cold," said Nat merrily, crossing her fingers behind her back. "But we'll HAVE to go to Oswald's wedding now, won't we?" said Nat. "Did you see what his chainsaw did to the heads of those flowers?"

Dad had that panicked look on his face that Nat recognised, the one he usually only got when Mum came home earlier than expected and the house was a mess and he was caught sitting in his Y-fronts on the sofa in front of the TV eating pork pies and pretending to write jokes.

"Oh heck, look, love, er, leave it to me. I'll think of something. Don't say anything to Tiffannee, OR – AND THIS IS WAY MORE IMPORTANT – your mum."

Nat had a great week at school that week, partly at the thought of not having to be a Perfect Fairy Princess Bridesmaid, and partly because Darius wasn't around much to ruin it. After a million warnings and about 600 red slips, he'd been sent to the Room of Doom, where the naughtiest kids at school got sent to cool off.

That wasn't the school's proper name for the room, of course. The proper name was:

The Super Happy Quiet Area and Time to Unwind Unit.

But everyone called it The Room of Doom, except for the kids who called it The Slammer. Or the Pit, The Cooler, The Hole, The Dungeon, or The Tomb.

Teachers just called it The Bagley Hotel.

Whatever it was called, it got shouty, twitchy, burpy, bogey-flicking Darius out of the way for a while, which meant Nat could enjoy the company of relatively normal human beings, like Penny Posnitch, Nat's best non-chimp friend.

"I don't know why you're making so much fuss about being a bridesmaid. I think you'd make a good bridesmaid," said Penny, on Friday lunchtime. "You should stop trying to get out of it. I'd love to be a fairy princess."

Yes, but you think you ARE a fairy princess anyway, thought Nat, shaking her head and smiling affectionately.

"No room can hold... *Darius the Super Ninja!*" said Darius, sneaking up behind the girls and dropping a woodlouse down Penny Posnitch's collar.

"EEEEW!" shrieked Penny, running off and leaving her shepherd's pie untouched. To be fair, everyone else's shepherd's pie was untouched too; it was rank.

Darius sat next to Nat and started shovelling down the leftover pie, eating quickly, with his mouth open.

Nat watched him and pulled a face. "It's like looking at a washing machine full of sick," said Nat, probably making it worse. The rest of the girls at the table fled too.

"Got rid of 'em for you," said Darius, "thank me later."

"I thought you weren't supposed to mix with normal kids this week?" said Nat. Darius just looked at her and grinned.

"Very funny," said Nat, realising what he meant.

"Your dad fixed up Oswald's wedding yet?" said Darius.

"Not yet, but I'm sure he will," she said.

"All the Bagleys are starting to arrive already, so I hope for his sake he will."

"They're not all as bad as Oswald, are they?" said Nat anxiously.

"Oswald's the black sheep of the Bagleys," said Darius.

"Oh that's good," said Nat, relieved.

"Yeah," grinned Darius, "he's the *good* one."

Nat smiled a thin smile.

"Don't forget, Buttface, when you get out of your cousin's wedding you owe me a favour. We still have a deal."

"Yeah, whatevs," said Nat. "As yet, Dad hasn't

had the courage to tell Tiffannee, which means I'm not out of it yet, which means I still have to go to her stupid Bridal Shower tomorrow."

"Remember the plan. Play along like you love it," said Darius, "then no one will know you tried to get out of it. Right, I'm gone."

He ran off as a furious Mr Frantz appeared, shouting.

"Vere did you go you terrible boy? Get back into ze Bagley Hotel, ach I mean ze slammer, no, the hole, ach, the happy Quiet box."

Dad's week was going way less well than Nat's. He had spent every waking hour so far trying to find a venue for a Bagley wedding, and wasn't having any luck.

"It's like I'm trying to organise the annual general meeting of the 'We love Mad Axemen Society'," complained Dad when Nat got home that night. There were dark circles under his eyes. "Plus there's a billion and one things to sort out still for Tiffannee."

Dad ladled out their pork pie and baked bean surprise dinner. Nat grimaced; *Mum's not in for tea then*, she thought.

"But why are you even still planning Tiffannee's wedding? Haven't you told her we're not going yet? Can't you just tell her now so I don't have to go to her stupid Bridal Shower tomorrow?" moaned Nat.

"I can't tell her, no, because there ISN'T a Bagley wedding yet," said Dad, "and there won't be unless I can find a venue that will have them."

Nat began to panic. "But you HAVE to find them a venue, Dad…"

"Yes, but on the other hand, if I find a venue for Oswald's wedding then you won't be able to be a bridesmaid at Tiffannee's wedding, and there'll be a terrible family row," he said. "And your mum will kill me."

Nat sighed. "Yes but—"

"—if I can't find a venue for Oswald's

wedding," interrupted Dad, "there'll be a terrible row with Oswald."

"And HE'LL kill you," said Nat. "In a WORSE way."

Dad rubbed his bald spot, a sure sign he was worried.

"Well we can't be in two places at once, Dad," said Nat lightly.

Dad paused, thinking hard.

Nat was going to regret saying that…

That night in her room, Nat went online to read about bridal showers. She knew the other bridesmaids would be there and didn't want to embarrass herself by not knowing what to do.

After an hour she turned her laptop off in disgust. Bridal showers, she decided, were UTTERLY LAME.

As far as Nat could make out, a Bridal Shower was a soppy little party just for girls. Everyone gets together and talks about how great the bride is and gives her even more presents and attention.

Getting married is like having your own personal Christmas, Nat decided.

What was filling her with horror was THE GAMES. Everyone was expected to play silly party games, and Nat thought that they all sounded really embarrassing. They were all about secrets, or making you do awful dares.

It was as if someone had invented the absolute worst kind of party and was making her go.

At least Mum will be coming, thought Nat. She'll look after me.

But when Nat heard the front door go later that night and Mum came in to say good night, she broke the bad news... Mum WASN'T coming.

"I'm truly sorry," said Mum, passing Nat a present for Tiffannee and not looking sorry one bit, "but I've been called away on very urgent business for a few days. I have to leave first thing in the morning. You know how it is."

Yes I do know how it is, Mum, Nat thought, crossly, *how it is that you* always *manage to get out of doing rubbish things.*

"Remind me, what is it you actually do, Mum?" asked Nat. Darius was convinced Mum was a spy, and every so often, Nat believed him.

"Oh, it's just boring old business," said Mum. "If I told you, you'd be asleep in two minutes. In fact, I'm boring myself just thinking about it. Boring boring yawn yawn."

"Does Dad know what you do?" Nat said, suspiciously.

"You father doesn't know what HE does," joked Mum.

Nat giggled.

Mum always made her laugh.

"You don't mind me going do you?" said Mum.

Nat shook her head and realised now she wasn't even fibbing; although she was worried about the bridal shower, she knew that the longer mum was out of the way, the more chance she had of achieving her plan of avoiding Tiffannee's fairy bridesmaid disaster.

"I have to say I think your dad's doing a pretty good job of the wedding so far," said Mum. "I know the family wanted ME to organise it, but perhaps we should all have a bit more faith in him."

"Interesting idea," said Nat.

"Now get some sleep," said Mum, "and I'll be back before you can say BRIDAL SHOWER."

Sleep? thought Nat, glumly, *with those bride-zillas waiting for me? I'll be lucky.*

CHAPTER TWELVE

· · · ·

THE BRIDAL SHOWER WAS BEING HELD AT CHIEF Bridesmaid Daisy Wetwipe's flat. Daisy opened the door to Nat and fixed her face in a TOTALLY FAKE smile.

"SOOOO glad you could come," fibbed Daisy, grabbing the present and shoving her through into the sitting room. "Look, everyone, it's lovely, super-keen, bestest assistant Chief Bridesmaid, Nathalia *Bumole*."

Everyone in the room laughed. Nat winced. She hated anyone knowing her horrible surname.

"It's pronounced Bew-mole-*ay*," she said. "It just looks funny written down."

This got even more laughs.

"Didn't I tell you she was totes hilarious?" said Annie Chicken, flashing Nat a mean smile.

If you lot were spies, you'd be found out in ten seconds, thought Nat glumly. *You're all rubbish fakes.*

Nat looked around the room. There were at least twenty women in the room, including the remaining bridesmaids, who were all wearing plastic tiaras with…

I'M A BRIDESMAID. 'MAID' FOR TROUBLE!

…printed on them.

Tiffannee, who was actually looking quite beautiful in a simple coral-coloured dress plonked a bridesmaid tiara on Nat's head.

"SO glad you came," said Tiffannee, giving her a squeeze. "And how's my favourite little fairy princess today?"

"Incredibly happy. Why are you asking, it's not like I'm trying to get out of it or anything," gabbled Nat, guiltily. She quickly poured herself a glass of orange juice and took a big glug. Tiffannee looked a little confused. "Oh, um, well that's good. Have you met everyone?"

Nat didn't recognise the other women, but guessed they were Tiffannee's friends, along with a smattering of those relatives who only appear at weddings and funerals. She was introduced to everyone. It seemed all Tiffannee's friends were called things like Indigo Sparkle and all the relatives were called Doris.

Pop music played from somewhere, and all the songs were about love, marriage or something ruder. The room was stuffed to the ceiling with super-girly decorations. There was a large table decorated with wedding ribbons and confetti and covered with finger food. There were shiny freshly-baked cupcakes, delicate sandwiches and chocolate-smothered treats. Nat thought the food actually looked quite delicious. She had forgotten to eat breakfast and her tummy rumbled.

Nat was offered a refill of her orange juice glass. She noticed that everyone else was holding glasses of champagne and that there were already quite a few empty bottles lying about.

You lot have started early, thought Nat, listening to the screeching as someone told a rather saucy 'wedding night' gag. Nat braced herself for a horrible day.

The room was crowded and everyone was busy gossiping and shrieking, but Nat saw a large empty cushion on the floor that looked comfy and away from most of the noise. She plopped herself down on it.

PAAARP.

It made a horrible, flabby trumpet sound. A trouser-trumpet sound, to be precise. All the women laughed and clapped and hooted.

"You sat on the fart cushion of truth!" squealed Indigo Sparkle.

Oh ha ha, very funny, thought Nat. *Very mature, I must say*.

"Tell us a secret, or do us a dare," chanted the girls.

"Have we started already?" said Nat, miserably. "No one said we'd started already."

"Truth or dare, truth or dare!"

Nat didn't want to risk taking a dare, not with the rotten bridesmaids here. They might dare her to dance in her pants on the roof or something. So she decided to tell them a secret.

She told them one of her MANY embarrassing Dad stories. She had loads to choose from. Nat was actually quite good at telling embarrassing Dad stories, because he'd been embarrassing her for a very long time.

She told them about the time Dad had demanded to come into the changing rooms with her at a big clothing store. He had had a massive row with the shop assistant because he'd said Nat was 'too little' to be left on her own.

"All the women ran out screaming," said Nat. "I was ELEVEN."

The bridal shower girls all fell about laughing.

"How *embarrassing*," said bridesmaid Annie Chicken

"He's *terrible*," said bridesmaid Tilly Saddle.

"Your dad is the *worst*," said Chief Bridesmaid Daisy Wetwipe. "He's so awful. He's the pits."

"Hang on," said Tiffannee, her smile fading, "that's a bit much. This is my *family* you're talking about. He was only trying to look after Nat."

There was a bit of an uncomfortable silence and Nat felt an unexpected stab of fondness for her silly cousin.

"Only kidding," said Daisy, a bit sulkily.

Soon the bridal shower was in full swing again, and Nat was almost enjoying herself now. She even felt a teensy bit guilty for trying to wriggle out of being a bridesmaid.

And she'd made a terrible deal with the devil – i.e. Darius – to do it. Somewhere Nat knew awful things were going to happen to her.

She imagined Darius, with horns, wreathed in red smoke, waving his litter stick at her and cackling:

YOU ARE THE WORST BRIDESMAID IN THE HISTORY OF THE WORLD, EVER!

"Shuddup!" said Nat out loud, getting lost in her vision, "I'm NOT a rubbish bridesmaid," just as the pop music stopped.

There was silence. Nat felt her cheeks glowing red.

"She's not," said Tiffannee loudly, staring reproachfully at the nearest bridesmaid to Nat, who happened to be Chief Bridesmaid Daisy, "and stop saying she is."

"I didn't say anything!" said Daisy. She dropped her voice and hissed at Nat, "You're at it again, trying to get rid of us. I'm on to you, missy, I really am."

Oops, thought Nat as the music and chattering started up again. *It's 'cos I'm hungry, I'm not thinking straight...*

She decided a cupcake and a ham sandwich might cheer her up. She was amazed none of the food had been touched; it looked so delicious. *Hmmm, I suppose they're all too busy glugging fizz*, thought Nat, filling a plate with tasty treats.

But as she took her first bite, the girls at the bridal shower leapt up shouting:

"She's the first, she's the first! Piggy piggy piggy! Oinky oink oinky!"

The rest of them rushed over to the table and starting wolfing the food.

Someone grabbed Nat and put a little piggy nose on her, kept in place by a bit of elastic that snapped on to the back of her head.

"Hey," said Nat, "that's not very nice. And OUCH, that stings."

"Sorry," laughed Daisy, "but it's just another

silly game. You can take the piggy snout off in an hour."

Tiffannee came over and hugged Nat. "I was starving," she said with a wink, "thanks for taking one for the team."

Nat just wanted to go home, but Darius had told her to play along until Dad broke the news to Tiffannee and so she pretended to laugh with everyone else. She even forced herself to make little oink-oink noises.

"She's such a good sport," she overheard Tiffannee saying to ex-First Assistant Bridesmaid Annie Chicken.

"Yes, that's what I said," said Annie through gritted teeth. "She's a real treasure."

Daisy sidled up to Nat. "And you know what happens to treasure, don't you?"

"It's – er – treasured?"

"No, it's *buried.*"

Nice, thought Nat, *really nice.*

She smiled at the bridesmaids as a wicked

thought struck her. *With a bit of luck Oswald Bagley will eat the lot of you.*

A little later and the food was all gone but the fizz bottles kept popping. The conversation had gone from a 12A rating (parental guidance required) to a 15 (not suitable for children, and may include VERY EMBARRASSING GIRL STUFF).

Nat felt a bit like she was watching a slow-motion car crash. She wanted to tear her eyes away, but somehow couldn't.

Women are just plain WEIRD, she thought. *I am NOT growing up, and I'm certainly not getting married. Even if boys weren't revolting, which they are.*

She was in the middle of this lovely conversation with herself when she heard the words:

"Let's play slumber party!"

"Yay!" shouted the other girls.

"Woo," muttered Nat.

"This one's a bit naughty," said Daisy giggling.

Ew, thought Nat.

"Have you all brought your jim-jams?" asked Chief Bridesmaid Daisy Wetwipe.

The girls all giggled and nodded.

"No," said Nat, loudly. "No one told me about this."

"She just doesn't wanna do it," said Annie Chicken with a smirk.

"Boo," said Tilly Saddle.

"Spoilsport," said Daisy.

"No, I do want to do it," fibbed Nat, feeling very uncomfortable. "I do, honest."

"She doesn't have to if she doesn't want to," said Tiffannee kindly.

"No, I'll have a go," said Nat.

"Fortunately, I have a spare pair of PJs," said Daisy.

Everyone cheered.

"Yay," said Nat, feebly.

The Chief Bridesmaid handed Nat a tiny pair of pyjamas with cute little teddy bears on.

"They're my kid sister's," said Daisy. "They might be a bit short, but you're skinny enough to wear them."

Gee thanks, thought Nat, sourly.

"Listen, ladies," announced Daisy, "here are the rules. I turn the lights out, and we all have to get changed into our 'jamas IN THE PITCH BLACK."

Everyone went: "Oooooh."

"The first one to do it shouts, 'Wedding night!' and the lights go on. Loser is the least dressed."

Right, well I'm not losing this, thought Nat, who had quite a competitive streak. *I'm not going to be the least dressed – how awful would that be?*

Tilly drew the curtains and the girls stood up, nightwear at their feet.

"Ready... steady... wait for it, Indigo... GO!"

The lights went out and the room was plunged

into darkness. Nat grabbed her teddy bear jim-jams in one hand and scrabbled out of her jeans in double quick time. Within seconds she had her top off and had squeezed herself into the tiny kid's pyjamas.

Nat was a whizz at getting dressed in the dark; Dad had blown the fuses in the house so many times she was used to it. As she did up the final buttons she reckoned she was ahead of the game. Yes! She was finished.

"Wedding night!" she shouted, sure of victory.

The lights went on.

She was the only person wearing pyjamas.

Tiny, fluffy, teddy-bear pyjamas.

For a second there was silence, and then the horror of the trick came crashing down on her. Then there was a screech of laughter from the horrible bridesmaids.

Nat knew she was going red and she felt like crying, but she wasn't going to let them see her upset.

"You're the most rotten bridesmaids ever," she said, "you're always talking about friendship and sticking together but you're selfish and mean."

She turned to the bride, who wasn't laughing.

"And that goes for you too, Tiffannee," she said, "you used to be really nice. I don't know what happened."

She turned and headed for the door, with as much dignity as possible.

Sadly, it wasn't very much dignity; she had both legs rammed down one trouser leg.

She bunny-hopped out.

Nat sat on the top of the stairs, waiting for the day to end and Dad to come and collect her. She wasn't sure how long she'd been sitting there but soon Tiffannee came to join her.

The bride-to-be put a gentle hand on her back.

"I'm really sorry about that," said Tiffannee quietly. "I am, honestly."

Nat muttered something under her breath. Mostly they were words that Darius had taught her, or that she'd heard Mum saying to Dad when he'd been especially annoying.

"I think they went a little too far," continued Tiffannee, "and I wish I'd stopped them. But you've been such a good sport the bridesmaids convinced me you wouldn't mind."

More muttering.

"Forgive me?" said Tiffannee.

Nat shrugged. There had been a couple of times today that she'd seen the old Tiffannee or Rosie – and here she was again. "S'pose."

"Thanks Nat. Do you really think I've changed?"

"A bit, yeah."

"It's this wedding," sighed Tiffannee, "I just get carried away sometimes. I so much want it to be—"

"Perfect, I know, yeah," said Nat. She really wished she wasn't starting to like Tiffannee.

Tiffannee smiled. "I think you must be the bestest bridesmaid ever."

Nat sat up and gave Tiffannee a half smile. "Can I go home now, please?" she said.

"Yes you can," said Tiffannee firmly. "You wait there. I'm calling a cab and I'm coming with you. As far as I'm concerned, this bridal shower is over."

CHAPTER THIRTEEN

. . . .

TIFFANNEE AND NAT DIDN'T SAY MUCH ON THE WAY home, but Tiffannee kept giving Nat's hand a little squeeze, which made Nat feel even worse. After all, she was still aiming to get out of being her bridesmaid. When the cab arrived at Nat's, Tiff gave her a peck on the cheek.

"Sorry again," she said, and then was gone.

Nat trudged indoors.

"Weddings are horrid and rubbish and I never want to go to ANY of them," she yelled, going into the kitchen.

Fiona was sitting there, calmly drinking tea.

"I hope you don't mean that," she said, "not about my wedding anyway."

"Ha ha, of course not!" said Nat, super-quickly.

"Your Dad was just about to tell me what he's arranged for us," said Fiona, pulling out her little police notebook. "You've had a week."

"Has it been a week?" said Dad. "Doesn't time fly when you're having wedding fun?"

Fiona looked at all the lovely bridal magazines that were lying about, and all the info about cars and flowers and decorations and she said: "I'm ever so impressed, you're obviously going to a heap of trouble."

Dad swept up all of Tiffannee's wedding stuff and squeaked, "No peeking!" in a slightly strained voice. "Something old, something new, something borrowed and definitely no peeking, that's the rhyme!"

Fiona shrugged. "So, where exactly are we getting married? It doesn't really matter as long as there's enough room for Merlin's cauldron."

Nat shivered. She knew Dad hadn't found anywhere.

"Not QUITE finalised that yet, lemme get back to you," he said.

Fiona licked her pencil. "And we all need to eat after the ceremony. Where are we having lunch?"

"Narrowing it down," fibbed Dad.

Fiona *chewed* her pencil. "And the party that night? The big Bagley bash. Where are we having that?"

"That's a massive surprise," said Dad.

There was a build-up of tension in the kitchen, but then...

"Did someone mention chips for tea?" called a familiar, hungry voice from the doorway. Bad News Nan barged in holding a big bag of chips above her head. Behind her, Nat could see Darius jumping up trying to get at them. Just like the dog.

"I was coming up the road and I saw little Darius. I thought I'd give him a hand," said Bad News Nan.

"She's eating them all out of the packet," said Darius. Nat saw the big tear in the chip wrapper.

"I had one tiny one, that's all," said Bad News Nan, "and then I got a bit of batter under the top plate of my teeth." She fished in her coat pocket, brought out her false teeth and handed them to Nat, who took the glistening gift with horror.

"Run them under the hot tap for a minute, will you, Nat?" said Bad News Nan.

By the time Nat had recovered enough to want to eat, the others were tucking into their chippy tea. Bad News Nan was talking about a funeral she'd been to recently.

After food, funerals were Bad News Nan's favourite topic of conversation.

"It was her wedding what killed Doreen Flipper," droned Bad News Nan.

"How did a wedding do that?" asked Fiona nervously.

"Doreen never liked her daughter Eileen's intended," said Bad News Nan, taking her teeth off Nat and attacking a bit of battered fish with gusto.

"Her heart gave out in the end, with all the strain. 'Course, it took another forty years for it to give out *properly*, but it got her in the end. Beautiful funeral, her son-in-law put on a lovely spread. I think she was wrong about him, but there was no telling her. Too late now."

"We're talking about HAPPY weddings today," said Fiona.

"Weddings always make *somebody* miserable, you mark my words," said Bad News Nan, happily.

"Yeah. Mainly me," muttered Nat.

"Well it's making *me* a bit miserable too, truth be told," said Fiona, and she looked so sad that Nat felt a rush of sympathy for her. "We're supposed to be getting married in two weeks and the only thing we're sure of is the cake. Oswald's mum's making it."

"Old Grammy Bagley?" said Bad News Nan. "You're letting *her* make your cake? Well, you're mad marrying Oswald, but if you let that woman near your cake you should be locked up in the funny farm."

"Why?" said Fiona, turning pale.

"Bowel-Basher Bagley we used to call her, down at bingo," said Bad News Nan with relish. She did the cakes for Arthur Teapot's ninety-fifth birthday. He never made ninety-six, that's all I'm saying."

Fiona looked upset. "I think I'm having pre-wedding nerves," she said.

"Listen to your nerves, they're trying to tell you something," said Dad, hoping she might call off the wedding.

"Don't listen to them," said Nat, hoping she wouldn't.

"Maybe you should put the wedding off for a bit," said Dad. "To next year even. Or the decade after. Long engagements are very fashionable. Ooh and then you could have it on a beach somewhere far far away abroad."

"What about Merlin and the giblets though?" said Nat, scowling angrily at Dad.

"Well exactly," said Fiona. "the giblets don't lie. It's now or never."

"Don't change anything. The wedding will be great. Everything will be fine EXACTLY AS PLANNED. Yum, lovely wedding," Nat added.

"Nothing's IS planned though, that's the problem – not the venue, the food, the party... not even the *cake* by the sound of it..." Fiona said.

"And Oswald's no help. All he wants to do is ride his horrible motorbike. I've a good mind to tell him it's me or the bike."

"I wouldn't give him that choice," said Nat.

"Everything's going wrong," said Fiona miserably.

And then burst into tears.

Why do weddings make everyone cry all the time? Nat wondered to herself as she got ready for bed that night. *They're supposed to be happy events, but I'm surrounded by people blubbing all the time.*

When Nat came downstairs to say goodnight to Dad he was still on his laptop failing to find a place for the Bagley wedding.

"Sorry I dropped you in this, Dad," said Nat, truthfully.

"It's OK," he said. "We just need our luck to change, that's all."

Just then the doorbell rang.

"Bit late for callers," said Dad, sounding puzzled as he got up to answer it.

Tiffannee was on the doorstep.

"The wedding's off," she said.

And then burst into tears.

Tiffannee was too upset to explain, she simply walked into the living room and put an American late-night news channel on. "Just watch," she snivelled.

Dad went off to make her a cup of tea while Tiffannee just blubbed on Nat's shoulder.

Eventually she heard something and looked up, pointing at the telly. "Look," she said.

It was a story from Texas. Four huge men in dark suits and dark glasses were shoving someone into a car.

"He looks a lot like your dad," said Dad coming back with the tea.

Nat sighed; Tiffannee's wailing got louder.

"Oh," said Dad, realising it *was* Tiffannee's dad.

The pictures changed to a big oil well, spewing oil all over the place.

"They're saying he might go to prison now,"

said Tiffannee, "he'll miss my wedding altogether unless he walks me down the aisle when I'm a hundred and six."

"Right. Kind of takes the pressure out of ordering these wedding centrepieces," said Dad.

Nat kicked him.

"No, that's it, I simply can't get married without Daddy being there," said Tiffannee. "So you might as well cancel it all… the venue, the food, everything. It's no use to me any more."

Nat saw Dad's eyes light up. And even though this was her dream come true, she had a horrible feeling she knew what he was now thinking.

"Oh dear," said Dad, trying to look sad but actually looking massively relieved, "never mind. But what a terrible waste. Such a shame nobody else could use them."

Nat was right. She DID know what he was thinking. Oh dear.

CHAPTER FOURTEEN

....

THE NEXT DAY DAD INSISTED THEY SHOULD 'STRIKE while the iron is hot' and tell Oswald and Fiona that they had finally found a venue for their wedding!

"Dunno what's so special about a hot iron," grumbled Nat, tumbling out of bed, "clonking someone with a cold iron is just as good."

"The Country Club won't know it's a Bagley wedding until it's way too late to cancel," chuckled Dad, when they were in the Atomic Dustbin, "ooh and I must remind Fiona to pretend to be called Tiffannee."

"This is insane," said Nat, "you do know that?"

"So's being in Oswald Bagley's bad books," said Dad, "remember the chainsaw?"

"You've got a point," said Nat.

"Brilliant," said Dad, totally cheerfully, "that's literally all the problems solved, it's a perfect plan.

"NOTHING CAN GO WRONG."

I wish you hadn't said that, thought Nat, *it always makes me nervous when you do*!

Then they went over to the Bagley house to break the good news.

Fiona was overjoyed when Dad told her about everything he'd so cleverly arranged for them at the posh country club.

"I've organised flowers and cars and food and entertainment and the lot," said Dad proudly. "I'm not saying it was easy, in fact most people couldn't do it, but *I couldn't let you down*."

He looked at Oswald when he said that. Oswald was sitting on his favourite chair in front of the telly, picking his teeth with a flattened beer can. He spat out the ring pull.

"Oh look, he's ever so grateful," said Fiona, smiling. "And so am I."

She threw her arms around Nat, who felt several of her ribs creak and groan under the strain.

"You and your dad have been so brilliant," she said. "Now Buttf— sorry, I mean Nathalia, I wanted to ask you something."

Nat feared the worst, quite rightly.

"You see, I never had a little sister, and all my friends are coppers and no good at this girly sort of thing, so I was wondering if you would consider being my… maid of horror."

"Honour," corrected Nat with a sigh, "it's maid of honour."

"Not at my wedding it's not," said Fiona.

"Merlin says that people need to embrace the darkness more. We need to cuddle our inner gloom to be truly happy."

"He'd like my mother," said Dad, "she's been cuddling her inner gloom for ever. Problem is, she keeps getting her inner gloom out to show everyone else as well."

Nat looked at Darius for help, but he just shrugged and made that twirly gesture with his finger next to his head, which meant: *dunno, she's bonkers, your call.*

"Would I have to wear anything weird?"

"What do you mean by weird?" said Fiona. "Are you saying we're weird?"

"Of course not," fibbed Nat, "not *weird* weird, just *different*. Am I going to have to wear anything *different*? The sort of different that some people – you know, some less 'New Age' people – might think was weird?"

"We believe in freedom," said Fiona. "Wear what you want. As long as it's black."

Nat broke into a huge grin. "I'll do it!"

"Wonderful," said Fiona, kissing her on the cheek. She let go of Nat who collapsed on the sofa, ribs aching.

Nat was actually looking forward to this wedding. Dad didn't like her wearing all black, he said it made her look like a fountain pen, but she thought it was dead cool.

"Now," continued the bride to be, "you do know *everything* has to be black, don't you?"

"That's easy, just tell all your guests to wear black," said Dad.

"Not just the guests," said Fiona, "I mean *everything*. Merlin was very clear about the black."

Flowers, cars, drinks, napkins, tablecloths, plates, even the food."

"Food?" said Nat, puzzled.

"I've done a suggested menu," said Fiona, handing her a note.

Squid ink soup
Blackened black angus beef with black pudding and
mushrooms de noir
Black forest gateau
Coffee (black) and chocolates (dark)

"Oh, er – I suppose so," said Dad, scratching his head.

Just then the doorbell rung, and a moment later Merlin Tolpuddle – wizard, astrologer, keeper of mysteries and dry-cleaning expert – entered. He was one of the most extraordinary looking men Nat had ever seen.

And that's saying a lot, she thought. *My life is full of nutters.*

She looked at Dad, who was wearing an old jacket and a ratty T-shirt with

I'M A TOP DAD

on it. Except there was a big tea stain down the front of it and some letters had come off in the wash so it read:

I'M A TOAD.

Merlin looked worse. He was clad in black and purple robes, with a long white beard, which he'd tied into a plait. On his head was a big floppy hat. He came into the sitting room and immediately sat down cross-legged on the floor, eyes closed, mumbling.

"Whoooooa…" moaned Merlin.

"He's checking out your aura," whispered Fiona.

"My WHAT?" said Nat, who didn't like the sound of that.

"Everyone has an aura; it's like energy," said Fiona. Nat giggled.

Fiona pursed her lips.

"It's no laughing matter," she said. "This is very important for my wedding. You are my bridesmaid of horror, don't forget."

"When you say 'horror'," asked Nat, suddenly feeling a bit nervous about the whole thing, "what exactly do you mean?"

Surely it can't be worse than fairy princesses, she thought.

"Oh, it's just an expression," laughed Fiona. "It's actually a nice thing. Merlin says we have to understand horror to understand loveliness. Like Oswald here."

"It's very deep," said Darius, "so deep some people think it's totally stupid and pathetic and all made up."

"THEN THEY WOULD BE WRONG!" intoned Merlin, in a loud booming voice. His eyes were shut tight.

"Everyone be quiet, he's in a trance state," said Fiona.

"He's definitely in a *state*," said Dad, quietly. Fiona shot him a sharp look.

"Sorry," said Dad.

Fiona carried on: "Merlin has created this wedding ceremony especially for me and Oswald. It's all about who we really are."

Should be interesting then, thought Nat, *'cos you're both really loopy.*

Merlin started chanting very loudly indeed.

"Hmmmm. Can I just ask, is this a wind-up?" asked Nat. "Only I've had a really bad time with a so-called joke at a bridal shower already and I'm not in the mood for any more teasing."

Fiona smiled and produced a huge shiny, silver wedding ring, engraved with strange writing. She handed it to Nat.

"Wow, Fiona, this is actually really pretty," said Nat, turning it round in her hand. "What's it made of, silver? Or is it white gold, or platinum?" It shone beautifully in the light. "I bet it's platinum."

"Nut tappets," said Fiona, showing Darius a similar ring.

"Ask a silly question," said Nat.

"They're from his bike engine," said Darius.

"Merlin says the rings should be made from something important to you," explained Fiona.

"Let's hope they're not important to the bike engine," joked Dad.

"Oh he won't be riding it any more. Oswald sacrificed his best, biggest and baddest bike for me," said Fiona.

"The beast?" said Darius. Nat saw even he was surprised. *Blimey, Fiona*, Nat thought, *you're tougher than you look.*

"Would you look after them for me, Nathalia, till the day?" said Fiona, almost shyly.

Nat felt surprisingly touched. "I'd be honoured," she said, and meant it.

Then Merlin stood up and poured a jug of cold water over her head.

"Hey, what the flip did you do that for, you

big beardy weirdy?" she yelled, hopping up and down. "I'm soaked through. Its running down my neck and it's on my jeans and AAARGH my pants are wet now!"

"The water stands for purity," said Merlin. "You are the ring bearer and must be pure."

Darius was chuckling like a baboon until Merlin took out a big fly swatter from his cape and started thrashing Darius with it.

"You are the Prince of Misrule and must be made pure," said Merlin, chasing Darius around the room.

"Can't I have the water?" he yelled. Now it was Nat's turn to chuckle.

"I must say, these new age weddings are pretty entertaining," said Dad, "you don't get this sort of thing at St Matthews."

Then Fiona darted towards Darius and gave him a heavy pair of rusty iron handcuffs to hold.

"Your job is to look after the cuffs of togetherness," she said, over the sounds of walloping. "Those were my grandfather's handcuffs," she added, proudly.

"I'm pure now," shouted Darius, "stop swatting,"

"Was he a convict?" asked Dad.

"No," said Fiona, crossly, "he was not. He was a copper. We've always been coppers, us Sweetlys."

"We've always been in show business," said Dad. "You know, entertainment runs in the Bumole's."

Nat winced.

"My grandad was in the movies," said Dad.

"Shuddup, Dad," said Nat, "he was not; he just worked at the Odeon."

"He was a cinema usher, OK, but he had his own torch and everything."

Fiona didn't seem very interested.

"You'll never guess who Grandad Sweetly arrested first," she said. "Go on, guess."

"Was it a Bagley?" said Nat.

"Oh," said Fiona, disappointed, "how did you know?"

"Wild guess," said Nat, quickly. "I picked a name at random."

"Ow ow ow," said Darius. Although less frequently as Merlin's arm was getting tired.

"It was Fingers Bagley," said Fiona, proudly. "Grandad caught him carrying a safe down the high road at midnight."

"Carrying it?" said Nat.

"Yeah," said Fiona. "Apparently he needed the money to buy a getaway car."

Nat thought about this for a minute. Then gave up. "Now, don't lose those rings," warned Fiona, "they mean everything to Oswald. I can't imagine what he'd do if you lost them."

Nathalia automatically fingered them in her pocket just to check they were still there. "I can imagine," she said nervously. Then a thought struck her.

"Fiona," she said, "you can't let Darius look

after those handcuffs for the next two weeks. He loses his pencil case during a lesson. He once lost his shoes, his jumper and his coat while Miss Hunny was taking the register."

"Let darling Oswald worry about that," said Fiona.

Nat looked over at Darius. Oswald had a huge hairy arm around him. Then he put the big iron handcuff around his young brother's grubby little wrist and snapped it shut. Before swallowing the key.

"That oughtta do it," said Nat.

CHAPTER FIFTEEN

· · · ·

At school the next day, Darius reminded Nat of their deal.

"You've escaped fairy princess bridesmaid doom," he said, "so you owe me a favour."

Nat was watching him pick up litter behind the science block. Wisps of smoke were still drifting from the science block, which was why he was picking up litter.

Something small and trapped scrabbled about in a bin. That's probably my soul in there, she thought, glumly.

"Favour time," said Darius, grinning.

"No way. You didn't get me out of it. You didn't cancel Tiffannee's wedding," she said, tartly. "Tiffannee cancelled it herself, so no deal."

"You shouldn't double-cross me, Buttface," said Darius.

"Get lost," she said. "Besides, your brilliant plan has got me tangled up in flipping Fiona and Oswald's weirdo wedding, which sounds almost as mad. Even if I can wear black for it."

Darius stood silhouetted in the smoke from the science block window, his scruffy hair sticking up from his head, like horns. He lifted up his litter-picking stick. It had three prongs, like a fork.

"Are you going to owe me a favour or not? Last chance."

An eggy smell, rather like sulphur, tickled Nat's nose.

"NO I AM NOT," she said, "so there."

Something like a clap of thunder shook the air.

Nat jumped in fright. But then she realised it was only the Atomic Dustbin, pulling up in the car park.

"Ha. That the best you can do? That's not very frightening," she said, going off to see why her dad was here.

It turned out that things were starting to get frightening after all. VERY frightening.

"What are you doing at school, Dad?" said Nat, bounding up to him in the car park. "You know I hate it when you come to school, you always embarrass me."

"It's nothing to do with you, young lady, stop worrying," said Dad cheerfully. Nat noticed he had his ukulele case under his arm.

Uh oh, she thought.

"We're rehearsing."

AAAAAAGH, she thought.

"Is this your stupid band?" she said. "Dad, I know you like to play and everything, but please just hire a real band for the Bagley wedding.

Penny Posnitch's auntie got married and I've seen videos of that band and they were ace. They knew proper songs. Songs that everyone likes. Songs in tune too."

"I couldn't hire a band even if I wanted to," said Dad.

"What do you mean?"

"I've been adding up the figures, you know, the costs of this wedding. Thing is, Fiona and Oswald haven't got as much money as Tiffannee, seeing as they haven't got an oil well, so by the time they've paid for hiring the Castle Country Club, there's nothing left over in the kitty for the little extras Tiffannee could afford."

"Little extras like what?"

"The cars, the flowers, the food, the photographer, that kind of thing," said Dad. Nat looked at him in horror.

"That's not little extras, Dad," she said, "that's massively lots of the wedding. What are you gonna do? You promised them a big wedding."

A few drops of rain fell.

"Don't worry, I've been thinking and I reckon we can do most of it ourselves."

"Well, you need to get started," said Nat, panicking.

"That's why I've called for an emergency band rehearsal," said Dad, happily. "You can play on a couple of songs if you like."

"I don't like," said Nat, "I don't like one tiny bit."

"The head has given me permission to rehearse in the music room," said Dad. "We have to practise right away. I don't want to embarrass myself in front of all those wedding guests."

"You are *not* going to play in the wedding band. Even if you rehearsed for ten years it's way too embarrassing and you're way too old and rubbish."

"There's nothing embarrassing about 'The Hunnypots'," said Dad. "We were the stars of our college, let me tell you."

"Please don't tell me..." said Nat.

"I would describe our sound as classic rock with a comedy twist," said Dad, walking towards the school entrance and smiling at the memories.

"Of course, we didn't start out with a comedy twist, but everyone used to laugh when we played, so we realised we were just naturally funny."

"You were naturally rubbish," argued Nat. "Mum told me that people used to throw bottles at you."

"Oh yeah, but the joke was on them because we got money back from the empties," said Dad cheerfully. "So who won, eh?"

"Even your name was stupid," said Nat. "I mean, 'King Ivor and The Hunnypots'?"

"It was clever," said Dad, "because Dolores Hunny was the lead singer."

An icy hand of doom crawled up towards Nat's heart. Dolores Hunny was the name of her English teacher. Who was also by some horrible twist of fate Dad's old college friend.

She knew this but what she hadn't known was something EVEN MORE HORRIBLE.

Her dad and her teacher were in a band together.

And now they were going to play at a wedding. In front of real-life people she knew. *Could anything in the world be more embarrassing?* thought Nat.

The icy hand grabbed Nat's heart, and gave it a proper old squeeze. In the back of her mind, she could hear Darius Bagley, cackling in triumph.

For the rest of the day, Nat told herself off for being silly. Of course it wasn't Darius's fault that Dad was at school trying to ruin her life; that was just silly. It was just a spooky coincidence.

A spooky, *terrifying*, coincidence.

She was so rattled that even dreamy Penny Posnitch asked her if she was feeling all right. And Penny never noticed anything. She never even noticed that time when Darius super-glued her plaits together.

"One more chance," said Darius, coming up behind Nat suddenly as she hopped into the Atomic Dustbin at hometime, and making her jump.

"NO FLIPPING DEAL," she answered loudly. Then she slammed the slidy door and said: "Dad, Darius says he doesn't want a lift tonight."

She stuck her tongue out at him as they drove off.

"I tell you what, we've still got it," said Dad as they coughed and spluttered their way home.

"What?" said Nat, crossly.

"The old showbiz magic," said Dad, "me and Dolores Hunny, we're still hilarious. And more than a tiny bit *rock and roll*, I can tell you."

Nat felt more than a tiny bit sick.

"You wait till we get 'Shredder' Boris and Dave The Tub Thumper back in the band," said

Dad. "We are gonna smash that wedding."

"It's a Bagley wedding, Dad," said Nat as they pulled up at home, "I think they can smash it for themselves."

"Yes, well we'll have to stop them," said Dad, "it's me who booked the golf club in the first place, it's me who'll have to cough up for any damage."

Nat hadn't thought of that. The day was getting worse.

But just when Nat thought things couldn't get any worse... they got home to find Tiffannee and Hiram sitting on the sofa, holding hands like a couple of love birds.

"We've got some great news for you, little lady," said Hiram.

Uh-oh, thought Nat.

"You tell 'em, honey," said Hiram.

"Daddy's lawyer called. He said the little oil spill probably wasn't Daddy's fault," said Tiffannee.

"Yay," said Nat, flatly.

"So he *should* be able to leave Texas very soon, and come to the wedding after all."

"The CANCELLED wedding," Nat reminded them. "The very sadly cancelled wedding, which you're not having any more."

"Well…" began Hiram.

"Also," gabbled Nat, who had a horrible feeling she knew what was coming, "what if your dad CAN'T make it? You can't take the chance. You really ever so much can't take the chance."

Hiram lifted up a massive laptop. "So that's why I bought *this*. Do you know the little old church we're getting married in has just got superfast broadband?"

Nat was confused. "So?"

Tiffannee squeaked with pleasure. "So even if Daddy *can't* make it in person, he said go ahead, he'll be there ONLINE."

"Ain't the modern world great?" said Hiram, beaming.

"In other words… THE WEDDING IS BACK ON!" said Tiffannee, clapping her hands. "My dream is alive! Come here and be hugged, I don't even care if you crease my dress!"

Nat began to sway dizzily as she was gripped in a squeezy hug. Tiffannee gave her loads of tiny, tickly kisses and Nat could see big fat tears of joy on her cousin's face.

"You've been such a big help," said Tiffannee, "even when I've been a bit stressy. Knowing I could always count on you has helped me through this. You two are the best family in the world… ever!"

Nat heard Dad gurgle something next to her, and Hiram say…

"Gee, you look a little pale…"

Outside, the rain lashed down.

Her last thought, as she slid to the floor, was that somewhere, there was a tiny evil Bagley, rubbing his hands in glee.

CHAPTER SIXTEEN

· · · ·

THE MOOD AS DAD DROVE NAT TO SCHOOL THE next morning was glum.

"Dad, what ARE you going to do about having TWO weddings booked in there AT THE SAME TIME?" said Nat, as they drove past The Country Club of Double-Wedding Doom, as Nat was now calling it.

"Leave it to me," said Dad.

He said the same thing when he picked her up that afternoon, only this time Nat could tell there was an extra note of panic in his voice.

"I've left it to you all day, Dad," said Nat, "I always leave things to you and it always ends really badly."

"Don't worry," said Dad "I'll get an idea soon-ish. I work better under pressure."

"We're in even more of a mess than before," said Nat. "There's nothing else for it, I'm gonna tell Mum what's happened, she'll sort it out."

Dad pulled up on the kerb with a screech. He turned to Nat. "Your mum is ever so good at sorting things out," he said carefully, "but so are nuclear weapons."

"What do you mean?" said Nat.

"In both cases, there's a lot of fall-out," said Dad. "Horrible, horrible fall-out."

Nat thought for a while. This was true. And she reckoned a little bit of that fallout might very easily reach her, in the circumstances.

"OK, well it seems to me you've only got two choices," she said.

"I know," said Dad, and then paused. "Remind

me what they are again."

"Choice one – you tell Oswald Bagley he can't have the big wedding party you've promised him."

"I don't like the sound of that."

"Choice two – you tell Tiffannee you've given her entire wedding to someone else."

"That sounds horrible too. What's choice three?"

"THERE ISN'T A CHOICE THREE, DAD, YOU SPANNER."

"Right," said Dad. "I'll think of a way out, don't worry. Just trust me and act like there's definitely not a horrible wedding disaster looming up ahead that's going to get us both killed – or worse."

When Nat got to school the next day she went to find Darius, who was picking up litter as usual. She had a feeling the school quite liked making Darius pick up litter as she reckoned it saved them thousands of pounds on having a proper cleaner.

"Come to say sorry?" said Darius, surrounded by crisp packets.

"Shut up and listen," she said, "or I'll tip all this litter out and you'll have to start again."

She told him how Tiffannee's wedding was now back on, but how they'd already given her posh wedding to Oswald and Fiona.

"You got what you wanted," said Darius. "If your cousin can't get married, you haven't got to be a fairy princess. You win."

"BUT I DON'T WANT TO WIN LIKE THIS," yelled Nat, utterly miserable. "I know she's a bit annoying, but she's quite sweet really."

And then she said the dreaded words that Mum and Dad annoyed her so by saying, but now really DID seem to explain everything:

"She's *family*."

Darius stopped jabbing at rubbish and looked at her for a long time.

"Family," he said eventually. "Yeah, I get it."

"I don't even care if I'm a stupid fairy princess any more," said Nat, feeling as low as she could remember. "I just want Tiffannee to have a nice wedding like we promised. But without scuppering Fiona's." She was expecting Darius to say it served her right for backing out of his evil deal, but he didn't.

"In science," began Darius, and Nat groaned. "In science," he began again insistently, "two things can be in the same place AT THE SAME TIME."

"What?" said Nat, who didn't like science lessons. Except when Darius blew them up.

"But only when you don't know where they are."

"I thought you might be able to help, you total chimp," said Nat, stomping off.

That day after school Darius was already in the Atomic Dustbin when Nat hopped in. Nat had a nasty feeling *Darius* could be in two places at the same time. Being naughty in both.

"Darius has had a BRILLIANT idea," shouted Dad. "We can save both weddings!"

Nat looked at Darius, but he was rolling about with the Dog in the back as usual.

"How?" asked Nat, suspiciously.

"You'll see," said Dad, starting up the campervan with a loud bang and pulling away.

Five minutes later, they were standing in a bit of waste ground on the outskirts of the town.

"See," said Darius.

"What?" said Nat, "a circus?"

"I do like the circus," said Dad, scolding Darius gently, "but I think I need to sort this wedding disaster out before we start enjoying ourselves."

In front of them was the rattiest, most run-down circus Nat had ever seen.

There was a red-and-white-striped big top that could only be described as a small top.

There were a cluster of empty booths with hand
painted signs saying things like:

THE GREAT GLADYS
Fortunes told – warts removed
2 for 1 deal

And:

PUNCHY MCGEE
KNOCK HiM OUT AND WiN FREE TEETH!

There were half a dozen scruffy ponies
wandering around looking for grass to nibble on,
but the ground was mostly bare and muddy.

A huge hand-painted sign on the big top said
in wonky letters:

Spiro Bagley's
Super Circus

"This is my uncle Spiro's Circus," said Darius. "He's over here for Oswald's wedding."

"It's not very super," said Nat, watching a large dog wee up the side of a unicycle. "In fact, it's manky."

Darius handed them an article he'd torn out of one of Tiffannee's bridal magazines. There was a big feature on 'Perfect Olde English Summer Fayre Weddings'. The picture showed a huge green lawn, chock-full of happy guests. In the middle was a beautiful big marquée.

"I don't get it," said Nat. "What's that lovely wedding got to do with this ratty old circus?"

"You need to use your imagination," said Darius.

"I get it!" said Dad, jumping up and down in happiness. "Darius, you're a genius!"

"I do not get it," said Nat, hopping up and down in fury. "What's going on?"

"We can do BOTH weddings at the same time!" said Dad.

"*How*?" said Nat.

Darius and Dad looked at her as if she was a small, dim child, or an especially thick spaniel.

"You tell your cousin you've got an even better wedding than the Country Club arranged for her," said Darius.

"Meanwhile we just tidy this place up a bit," said Dad, "and in no time we'll have the place looking like a perfect wedding summer fayre."

"That way Oswald and Fiona keep the Castle

Country Club for their wedding," said Darius.

"And if we time it right we can run backwards and forwards between the two weddings…"

"And be at both at the same time," said Darius.

"And no one will be any the wiser!" finished Dad, putting his hands on his hips triumphantly. "Simple. What can possibly go wrong?"

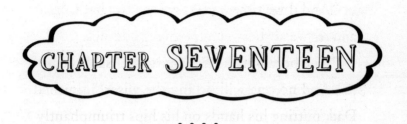

CHAPTER SEVENTEEN

• • • •

NAT STARED AT DAD COLDLY. SHE HAD HEARD THAT line WAY too many times.

"A MILLION things can go wrong, Dad!" shouted Nat. "The cars, the flowers, the food, the cakes, the band, the disco, the whole thing…"

"That's just *details*," said Dad, "we've got days to get that together."

"Easy," said Darius.

"I think this could be just what Tiffannee wanted," said Dad.

"She wanted *traditional*," said Nat. "Ye olde

English traditional. I don't think she wanted acrobats, fire eaters, trapeze artists and lion tamers."

"No lion tamers," said Darius. "That's banned these days. It's cruel, and besides, the lion ate the tamer."

"Shame. We could have fed the bridesmaids to the lions," said Nat.

They walked around a bit more. No one seemed to be about. Signs creaked in the breeze.

"Looking on the bright side, there's plenty of space," said Dad, "and we could call the big top a marquée."

"I suppose," said Nat, turning to Darius, "but are you sure we can borrow it?"

"You'll need to ask nicely," said Darius.

They walked a little further and saw some empty cages looking a bit sad.

"What does everyone do instead of lion taming then?" said Nat, who was still imagining Daisy Wetwipe being chased by a big, peckish cat.

"We had to learn the new tricks," said a large man with a big, bushy beard who suddenly appeared before them looking worryingly like Oswald Bagley. Except he was smiling and Oswald never did. The man had emerged from a weather-beaten blue caravan. He grabbed Darius and picked him up with one enormous hand.

"Alley-*oop*!" said the man and chucked Darius straight up like he was tossing the caber. Darius did a neat somersault and landed on the man's other hand.

You are literally a chimpanzee, thought Nat.

"We make a circus clown of you yet!" said the man, smiling. He held out an enormous hand the size of a dinner plate to Nat and Dad in turn. "Spiro Bagley," he said, "or – to use my full title: 'Spiro The Magnifico'."

Spiro The Magnifico bowed so low his twirly moustache almost scraped the ground. For a big man he was surprisingly bendy, thought Nat.

"Please be welcome to my humble home,"

he said, gesturing towards the largest caravan Nat had ever seen. It was wooden, raised high on huge wheels and had a carved, curved roof. It was painted red and white and there was a little chimney stuck on the top.

"When I was a boy," said Spiro The Magnifico, walking then towards the van, "it took four elephants to pull this caravan. Whole towns would come to a stop to watch it pass. Children would run in front waving the flowers for free tickets, and gardeners would run behind waving shovels, for the free manure." He sighed, "It's not same on the back of a lorry. Still, that's progress."

Inside it was warm and cosy, cluttered with sparkly cushions, thick rugs, shiny trinkets, bits of circus equipment, dogs, cats, a turtle named Desmond, three parrots and a penguin.

Spiro magnificently put the kettle on and Nat quickly realised that Dad had fallen in love with the caravan, probably because it was even older and fuller of junk than the Atomic Dustbin.

"I think of myself as a bit of a traveller too," Dad began. Nat flashed him a "shuddup," look that he ignored.

"I've got my own van," Dad burbled on, scratching the penguin's feathery head. "I've been everywhere in it."

"A fellow traveller," beamed Spiro. "Tell me, what do you think of Samarkand? Aren't the dawns the greatest thing? And midnight under the stars in the Atlas mountains? Makes you feel alive and free. And tell me, do the Kalash of the Rumbur valley still sing and play in the Hindu Kush?"

"I expect so," said Dad, "I once got stuck in a car park in Eastbourne and a minibus full of angry pensioners chased me up and down the sea front for hours. That was pretty life-changing. You don't wanna be on the receiving end of those zimmer frames, let me tell you."

There was silence. Nat looked for the biggest

cushion to hide under.

"Anyway, now we've swapped traveller's tales," said Dad, "I feel we're brothers of the road. So can we borrow your circus next weekend?"

Uncle Spiro laughed, magnificently, and handed out tiny cups of sweet tea.

"You make the big joke," he said, "you cannot do this, it's far too precious."

Nat looked out of a window. A lone dog howled and the sign fell off the fortune-teller's van.

"Leave this to me, kids," whispered Dad. "Go outside and play. Lemme talk to him, mano to mano."

Dad shooed her and Darius out, where they instantly bumped into a creaky old acrobat called Spangle Bagley who told them about how her arthritis played havoc with her high-wire act these days.

Spangle invited them into her caravan. Nat followed. Darius, bored, just wandered off.

Inside the van, Nat noticed it was covered with pictures of a young boy. "That's my son; he ran away from the circus to join a bank," she sniffed. "A bank, what kind of a dream is that for a young Bagley? We haven't spoken since."

When Nat came out again, Darius had properly disappeared.

It took her AGES to find him skulking around the back of the big top, next to a MASSIVE CANNON.

A sign next to it said:

FLATHEAD BAGLEY HUMAN CANNONBALL

Darius was climbing in. Nat giggled until she saw the fuse. It was alight! Darius had lit the fuse!

"What are you doing?" she yelled. "Come out of there, AT ONCE."

"Why?" said Darius. "I've always wanted to do it."

The fuse hissed further down. Nat ran over and tried to blow it out, but it just made it hotter.

"Get a *properly quick* move on," she yelled. "You might now have even less time than you had before I tried to put the fuse out."

"I wanna do it," said Darius, "get lost. Anyway, there's a safety net – look."

A gust of wind caught the nearby safety net. It collapsed.

"THE SAFETY NET HAS FALLEN DOWN!" yelled Nat.

"You could have told me," said Darius, scrabbling around inside to get out.

"Stop moaning, get climbing."

"I'm stuck," he said, scrabbling some more.

"That's 'cos you've spent a month in our pantry eating all our food, you greedy little chimp," said Nat.

"You're being fatt-ist," said Darius.

"No I'm not, just get your massive ugly backside out of there before you're blown up," shouted Nat.

But all she could hear was the sound of a small, wedged boy, wriggling frantically.

And the fizzing of a fuse.

I don't believe I'm doing this, thought Nat, and quickly ran up the cannon's steps and dived head first into the mouth of the huge gun.

"Grab my arms," she said. She felt two sticky hands grasp hers. She pulled, he pushed.

"Does this count as a favour?" she asked.

"What?"

"Is this the favour? The favour you think I owe you – even though I don't? Or shall I leave you in here?"

"Oh, I suppose so," said Darius.

Finally, agonisingly slowly, she hauled him out towards the lip of the big gun.

"One last push," she cried, and then they were both out, tumbling on to the ground.

"It was probably broken anyway," said Darius. Just then the cannon went off with a massive *BOOM* that brought Dad, Uncle Spiro and Gladys the fortune teller running over in a big panic.

"AAAAGH!" Dad shouted, seeing the smoking cannon and the two children lying on the grass.

"We're fine," said Nat, sitting up, as Dad fainted.

Gladys invited them all back to her tent for a hot cup of tea. Dad soon had a tartan blanket over his shoulders and the old lady making a big fuss over him.

Nat thought that wasn't very fair, as it was her and Darius who had just escaped cannonball doom, not stupid Dad. But she didn't say anything as she knew she was in MASSIVE TROUBLE for messing with the huge gun.

"I can see your future," said the fortune teller, peering into Dad's bloodshot eyes.

"I can see their future," growled Dad, looking at the children, "and it's a very unpleasant one, full of pain, suffering, early bedtimes, no suppers and no TV apart from historical documentaries."

Darius and Nat looked at each other. Neither of them had seen Dad this angry before.

Spiro bustled in, bent down and smothered Nat with kisses. "You are a brave little princess, you save the little monster, how can I thank you? Anything you want, you can have ANYTHING."

Nat didn't have to think for long.

"Can we borrow your circus?" said Nat.

CHAPTER EIGHTEEN

• • • •

THE WEEK BEFORE THE WEDDINGS WAS AS BUSY as any Nat could remember. She'd never seen Dad so manic, even when he was super-late delivering his rubbish Christmas cracker jokes.

There was SO MUCH to organise.

Firstly, they had to convince Tiffannee and Hiram that the new olde English country garden marquée picnic wedding was EVEN BETTER than the Country Club.

Dad was a terrible liar, so asked Nat to do it for him, and Nat asked Darius to help her. He was brilliant at lying.

"We've been so lucky," said the tiny evil fibber. "It's the same wedding tent as used by Her Majesty for last year's Royal Garden Party."

"Wow," said Tiffannee.

"Wow to the MAX," said Hiram.

"If it looks a bit like a big top, that's because her Royal Highness used to be a lion-tamer in the Royal Gardens," said Dad.

Nat kicked him. "Told you I was rubbish," said Dad, later.

Nat reluctantly agreed to learn how to play 'the wedding march' on the school piano, for some reason. Dad said it was part of a very clever and crafty Darius masterplan.

"It's something about giving you an excuse not to be where you should be so you can get somewhere else," said Dad, "it's terribly clever."

"You don't understand his masterplan, do you?" said Nat.

"Not all of it, no," said Dad.

The next thing Nat had to do was find someone daft enough to cook lunch for the Bagley wedding, as Fiona and Oswald couldn't afford to pay for the Country Club's catering.

Luckily, Nat knew a chef. Penny's dad, Mr Posnitch, a tiny little man from somewhere in Eastern Europe Nat couldn't pronounce, used to run his own restaurant. He also used to be a footballer, but that skill was less useful to Nat right now.

He was thrilled to be asked to cook, especially when Nat told him that Penny was going to be the guest of honour at Oswald's wedding. Just because they'd heard everyone in town saying how great she was. Nat knew enough about proud dads to know that this terrible porky pie would work.

Nat did get punished for her fib though – Penny asked her twenty times a day to repeat how great people thought she was for at least a week.

Dad was sorting out the catering and the photographer for Tiffannee's wedding, while Nat was organising the flowers for the bouquets, her one proper official bridesmaid job.

Darius had volunteered to be DJ for the night at both parties. He liked DJing because he could finally make as much racket as he wanted without getting sent to sit outside the Head's office.

His masterplan involved a clever schedule with routes and times and plots and plans so that they could all go to both weddings, more or less at the same time, without anyone noticing.

"Then when Darius has got everyone warmed up, it'll be time for 'King Ivor and the Hunneypots'," Dad kept reminding them, plucking his rubbish ukulele, "although we're only a duo now 'cos the drummer and guitarist reminded me they never wanted to see me again after all the boos and spitting and bottling at our last gig."

There was so much going on Nat decided to

write one of her famous lists. This one was titled:

WHAT I NEED TO WORRY ABOUT

1. Being in big family trouble forever for putting Tiffannee's perfect wedding in a Bagley circus tent in a muddy field.

2. Being chainsawed by Oswald if his wedding goes wrong.

3. Selling my soul to Darius.

4. Being in two places at the same time because it IS IMPOSSIBLE, no matter what Darius says, the little chimpy monster.

5. Dad being in charge of the Tiffannee wedding food.

6. Dad being in charge of the entertainment.

7. Dad being in charge of anything.

8. King Ivor and the Hunnypots – live!

9. Mum finding out.

10. Mum finding out.

11. Mum finding out.

That last one was SO terrifying Nat reckoned it counted as a treble worry.

With a rising sense of alarm she realised her original fear – the fairy princess bridesmaid dress – no longer even made it into her top ten!

Every day after school for the next few days Nat, Dad and Darius went down to the circus, which was slowly being transformed.

Nat had thought it would be impossible, but seemingly nothing was too much trouble for the girl who had saved little Darius Bagley. She was fussed over by arthritic acrobats and Gladys the Fortune Teller, while Dad and the rest of the circus folk scrubbed, cleaned, repaired, painted and generally transformed a manky old big top into a gleaming wedding venue! At the end of the week it was fit for a REAL princess, never mind a pretend fairy one.

"It's amazing," said Nat, the night they finished. "I can't actually believe it."

And she wasn't even fibbing.

The top was shining pink and gold, wild roses

were entwined with the guy ropes, and above the entrance someone had painted

ROLL UP! ROLL UP! WEDDING TONITE! ADMISSION FREE

Nat thought that was a nice touch. Even if it was spelt wrong.

Mum rang every night. Her business deal (or, according to Darius, her secret fight against agents of darkness) was at a tricky stage, she said, so she couldn't get away.

Darius said actually she was probably still trying to escape from an island doom bunker guarded by robot monkeys, until Nat pinched him several times and told him to stop worrying her as she was starting to believe him.

Mum was now going to fly back on the night

of the wedding. "I'll be there for the first dance," she told Nat. Nat and Dad decided not to mention that there were now TWO weddings that day because Dad said she might get a bit upset and it could spoil her business concentration. Nat said they should at least tell her that Tiffannee's wedding was going to be at a circus and Dad said he DEFINITELY would, but nearer the time, so as to cut down on the shouting.

Finally, it was the night before the weddings. Tiffannee came to stay at their house, adding to the double wedding secrecy and stress. Dad, who knew he was rubbish at keeping secrets, came over all dizzy and said he needed an early night.

"And now the weather report says freak storm expected," he whispered to Nat. "I think the picnic on the lawn might be tricky."

"Have you made the picnic?" she asked.

"Oh flip," he said. "I knew there was SOMETHING I'd forgotten."

"Dad!" yelled Nat, then, remembering to keep her voice down, "we have to give them a big posh lunch. You can't just hand out a dozen pork pies and say tuck in."

"All the shops are shut now," said Dad.

"I'm actually leaving home and I'm not even kidding," said Nat.

Dad dived into the big chest freezer and starting chucking stuff out. Big chunks of solid meat slid across the kitchen floor.

After a few minutes he said: "Right, that's all of it. What can we make with that?"

"We?!"

"Come on love, this is slightly your fault you know."

"Yes I know, don't remind me," grumbled fairy queen bridesmaid Nat, "lemme get a cookbook."

It was late when they eventually got to bed, having made great vats of 'Dad Stew' until the pantry was bare and Nat and Dad were both exhausted.

It's impossible, thought Nat, as she turned her light out. *THIS WHOLE IDEA IS IMPOSSIBLE.*

But as much as Nat didn't want to speak too soon, things did seem to have at last fallen into place...

When Nat awoke the next morning, it was to birdsong, and early morning sunlight filtering through her curtains. And Dad in the driveway kicking the van and swearing.

Nat couldn't quite believe it. But it was true. After all these weeks of planning, and all the madness and upset and mix-ups and confusions, here they were.

D-Day.

The day of the wedding.

The TWO weddings. The double bridesmaid disaster day, as she was calling it.

Nat's heart was already starting to beat quickly

as she rubbed sleep from her eyes and studied her big wall chart. On it was Darius's running order, and it was timed like a military operation. In fact, she reckoned one small war probably took less planning than two big weddings.

There was also a to-do list for the big day. It was long and terrifying. She had given a copy to Dad a couple of days before, along with strict instructions to memorise it. She guessed he must have at least read it because the first thing written there was:

MAKE SURE THE ATOMIC DUSTBIN WORKS.

Smoke trickled in through her bedroom window. For most people that might have been an alarming start to their morning, but Nat knew it meant the van was actually about to work. Sure enough, a moment later there was a familiar ear-splitting cough and a happy woof from the dog as the Atomic Dustbin rattled to life.

"It's gonna be a GOOD DAY!" shouted Dad, over the racket.

I wish I could believe it, thought Nat, I really do.

CHAPTER NINETEEN

· · · ·

OVER A HASTY BREAKFAST, DAD RAN THROUGH THE plans for the day, like a military general. Or rather, a hapless idiot pretending to be a military general.

"Remember," he warned, "at no point must Tiffannee – or your mum, if she gets back in time – know what we're doing. There might be unpleasant consequences."

"It's like black ops," said Darius, who had stayed over.

"What?" said Nat, munching her toast quickly.

"Secret missions," said Darius. "Spies, machine guns, grenades."

"Perfect," said Nat. "Shall we put those on the checklist then? Confetti, rings, flowers, machine guns, grenades."

There was a banging at the door.

"It's the bridesmaids come to get Tiff ready," said Dad, peeking out of the curtains. "Hide all the secret plans!"

Tiffannee ran down the stairs to greet her fairy princess bridesmaids. She was in a fluffy dressing gown, face slathered in cream, curlers in her hair. When she opened the door they all squealed.

"There's so much to do!" said Tiffannee shrilly, sounding way beyond stressed.

I see Tiffannee the Bridezilla is back, thought Nat, sourly. *Brilliant. This'll make the day so much easier.*

The bride went on. "My hair my nails my make-up my everything my— *aaaarrgh!*"

The last sound was made while pointing at Annie Chicken, whose face was bright red and covered with spots and flaky skin. She looked like she'd caught a disease from the middle ages like the scrofulous pox or something.

"Oh no, can you still tell?" said horrified Annie, putting her hands up to cover her face. "I put some concealer on."

"It needs more than concealer," said Darius as he walked past. "You could try a paper bag."

Annie burst into tears, and Daisy chased Darius up the stairs, trying to bash him with the heel of a shoe.

"You little monster," she yelled.

"No, I'm the monster," said Annie, sobbing.

And it had to be said, she did look a bit monstrous.

"I'm allergic to daffodils," she wailed. "Everyone knows that, but look what came yesterday."

She showed Tiffannee a big bouquet. Of daffodils, mostly. Annie Pox-face Chicken slammed them down on a side table, angrily.

"Nathalia was in charge of the bouquets," she hissed. "She did it on purpose! And it's worked. She's got her way – AGAIN. I can't come to your wedding like this." And she rushed out of the house in floods of tears.

"Nat, are you really still trying to nobble the

bridesmaids?" said Tiffannee. "And if you are, please stop it. It'll ruin my perfect day."

"I PROMISE I'm not!" said Nat, totally truthfully. She chose daffodils because they were free – she'd pinched them from next door's garden!

"I do believe you, truly I do. Just please stop it. Now come on, my last remaining fairy princesses, it's time to get ready!" said Tiffannee, as she and Daisy and Tilly ran upstairs squealing loudly again.

Nat followed, then ducked into her bedroom as she passed it.

She yanked the horrid fairy princess outfit from the wardrobe and sulkily put it on. She looked at herself in the mirror and felt properly sick.

Then she put her black dress and black jacket over the top to see how it fit. She could just about get them on. She looked lumpy, and she was already too hot, but it was an improvement at least.

By the time Tiffannee's carriage had arrived, Nat was a fairy princess again, though she left her big black boots on as they were a massive faff to get off, and were pretty much hidden by her long fairy princess dress anyway.

"Ready to go?" shouted Dad from downstairs.

Nat clomped down and waited for the others.

Then she saw Tiffannee.

She looked BEAUTIFUL.

She was wearing an incredible, long, straight white dress, simple and elegant. She had a crown of wildflowers and her hair was tumbling down in ringlets, framing her perfect face.

"Do I look all right?" said the nervous bride as she stepped lightly down the stairs.

"You look like an angel," said Nat, and meant it. "Are you sure you're related to Dad?"

Tiffannee smiled. "Here we go!" she said, as she walked out of the door, her bridesmaids following behind her.

Nat was relieved to see that Uncle Spiro had made the horse and carriage look absolutely gorgeous. The four circus ponies were proudly decked in blue and white ribbons and Nat reckoned the big plumes looked brilliant. She was less sure about the two creaky lady acrobats standing on their backs, but Tiffannee just clapped and laughed.

"Oh, I can see today's going to be full of surprises!" she squealed, then turning to Nat. "I want to thank you and your dad for making this day so perfect."

Don't say that yet, thought Nat, *it's not even 10am.*

But she had to admit things did seem to be going well. Even Dad looked nice, in a smart grey and black morning suit and top hat. He'd showered and shaved and looked quite human.

As opposed to Darius, who still looked like a goblin, even though he was now a goblin in a tiny black suit.

Dad and Nat now had to get to Fiona to start her day off, so they'd worked out a clever excuse for not going in the carriage with Tiffannee and the bridesmaids.

"Nat's got a special bridesmaid surprise for you," said Dad, "so we need to go on ahead. See you at St Michael's."

St Michael's? thought Nat. *I was sure it was St Mary's…* but she quickly forgot as Tiffannee kissed them all goodbye, and everyone waved and squealed excitedly as the carriage horses whinnied and the bride was pulled away. Ten minutes later and the Atomic Dustbin slowed down outside Fiona's house, just enough for Nat and Darius to leap out and get the bride. Nat had her black Maid of Horror outfit on top again.

"These wings have given me the hump," she said.

"Stop complaining," said Darius.

"No, I mean a real hump," she said.

Fiona came to the door looking like a pretty

vampire in a tight black leather and lace outfit. She tottered to the van in high-heeled shiny boots.

"You look fantastic," she told Nat. "Thank you so much for making my day so perfect."

I do wish everyone would stop saying that, thought Nat.

They dropped Fiona off at the park where she was meeting Merlin to go over the finer points of the ceremony, giving them enough time to gun it back to the church for the fairytale wedding.

"It's going well so far!" said Dad as they pulled up outside the church, which had a crowd of people gathered outside. "You hop out and get playing, I'll park somewhere. Hmmm, I can't see anyone I recognise yet."

Nat, in full fairy princess costume, clomped her way through the crowd. There were a lot of people wearing black, and lots of people were sniffing and dabbing their eyes with hankies.

Why does EVERYONE cry at a wedding? Nat

thought, stomping her way up the little stone steps to the balcony where the church organs always were.

I know people DO blub, she thought, *but this is ridiculous.*

She was so stompy, she completely missed a little sign near the front door with the order of service on. It said:

In memoriam.

CHAPTER TWENTY

· · · ·

IN THE BALCONY OF THE CHURCH, THERE WAS A very ancient man sat at the organ wearing a big white cloak. He was peering at the music and playing something a bit gloomy.

Flipping heck, people need to lighten up, thought Nat. *This IS a wedding, after all.*

"I do wish there was more light in here," said the organist. "Oh, hello little girl," he smiled in a kindly way. "Are you supposed to be an angel?"

"Nah, fairy," she said. "Tiffannee's the angel."

"I suppose she is now, yes, my dear," said the

man. "So, how are you feeling?"

"Stressed," said Nat, "really miserable and stressed. But I reckon it's all my own fault."

"It's not your fault," said the old man firmly. "But of course it's not unusual to feel like that at these times." He had such a lovely soothing voice Nat thought she might cry.

"It's been a horrible time," she said, sniffily.

"Of course. Have a hanky."

She took it and blew her nose.

"I mean, I know some people are happy about it."

"Happy? Are they? Ah, that's quite unusual."

"Oh yeah, you should hear them. But that's 'cos they don't know about the work that goes into these things. They just want a big party at the end."

"Party?" said the man, shocked now.

"That's all they care about. But we've been planning this for months."

"Planning? Who's been planning it?"

"Mostly me and my dad," said Nat, "but Darius has helped, the little monster."

"Monster? I hope you don't mean that," said the man, looking worried.

But by now Nat had plonked herself down at the keyboard and wasn't listening.

"Budge over," she said, "let's liven this up."

"Stress, I suppose," said the organist to himself. He looked over the balcony. "I think the car is here. Stay strong, little girl."

"A one, a two, a one two three four…" said Nat, brightly.

"Not THAT strong," muttered the organist.

Dah, dah dee-daaaah, Nat bashed out.

It was a very familiar tune. "Here comes the bride," sang Nat, "two metres wide…"

She heard a murmur of voices from the congregation below. Angry voices.

"What are you doing?" said the organist.

"It's the tune she wanted," said Nat, bashing the chords out.

"Are you absolutely sure it's appropriate?"

"Do you think it should be more lively?"

"Lively?"

"Yeah, to get everyone in a good mood early. I think people take these things way too seriously."

"That's because it *is* serious," said the organist. "I can't think of anything much more serious."

"Nat, Nat!" said Dad, running up the stairs. "Stop playing, you've made a mistake."

"Oh come on, I'm not that bad," said Nat, firmly. "It's about time I enjoyed myself," she said to the organist, "it's been making me ever so miserable."

"You're supposed to be miserable today, you wicked child!"

But Nat wasn't listening. She pressed her foot on the volume pedal and drowned out the man's words.

"DA DA DA DAAAAAH!" Blared the organ. Now there were shouts from below.

"Tough audience," shouted Nat, who was

loving the deep rich sound of the organ.

"Get off there," said the organist, grabbing her shoulders.

"What is your problem?" shouted Nat. "Gerrof me."

"Have some respect, remember, THIS IS A FUNERAL."

"Nat," said Dad, now at the top of the stairs, "it's the wrong church."

Nat made a strange, strangulated, squealing noise, taking her hands off the keys like they were made of molten lava. She jumped up and ran past Dad down the tiny spiral stairs out into the sunlight through the churchyard.

And straight into a hole in the ground.

A hole in the ground?

Who digs a hole in the ground?

Why would anyone, she spluttered, spitting gritty bits of earth out of her mouth, *why would ANYONE leave a dirty great hole in the ground?*

In a churchyard.

At a funeral.

Then she understood.

"AAAAAARGH!"

she shouted, scrabbling out in terror. **"AAAAARRRGH!!!!!"**

"What's the matter?" came a man's voice.

""G-g-grave! Grave. I fell in a grave," yelled Nat, who now had a tulip growing out of her head.

"That's not a grave," laughed the gardener, leaning on his spade, "it's just where I'm digging a new flower bed."

"Oh," said Nat, pulling herself together. "Then I am sorry to trouble you, good sir."

She walked stiffly out of the churchyard.

"Could have gone better," she said as Dad grabbed her and bundled her into the Atomic Dustbin.

Within minutes they were outside St Mary's church. Darius was reading over the wedding checklist.

"What about the photographer?" he said. "You know, the mad woman, does wars."

"I'd forgotten about her," said Dad, "but she's been booked, I'm sure of it."

"Clara Bonkers? Didn't Tiffannee sack her?" said Nat. "I thought you were going to hire someone else."

"No, I hired her back," said Dad, "I thought she was good. But I don't think she's confirmed. Check my emails," he said chucking his phone to Nat while he parked the van. "I'm a bit behind on them."

Nat did a quick search. "Great, Clara the loony photographer emailed you last night, really late," said Nat.

"Phew," said Dad. "I expect she was just writing from a local restaurant or something, saying she'll definitely be here today and there wasn't any need for me to worry?"

"No," said Nat, "she wrote the email from inside a tank. She says it all kicked off again in that place where it always kicks off and she'd rather take her chances with the SAS than with horrible bridesmaids and a vomity goblin."

"Does that mean she won't be taking the pictures?" said Dad.

"I know she's got a long lens dad, but she can't see us from inside a tank IN ANOTHER COUNTRY."

"Oh heck, so we need to get Tiffannee a photographer," said Dad, as he turned off the engine. A small group of excited wedding guests were milling about outside the church, all dressed up in bright sunny outfits; big hats and flouncy dresses, or smart suits with big colourful buttonholes. Plenty of them had cameras.

"I mean, this is ridiculous. Everyone takes pictures these days, everyone's got a camera. We must be able to find someone around here to take a few pictures."

"It can't be anyone she knows though, Dad," said Nat as they got out of the van, "it has to look like we've got a professional."

An elderly tourist with a large camera was strolling past.

"Hello," he said, "I am Henrik Henriksson from Norway, pleased to meet you."

"Um, pleased to meet you too," said Dad, "must dash, organising a wedding, sorry."

"I overhear you need picture? I come from Norway, taking the pictures of the pretty churches. I take pictures for you, yes?"

"Yes!" said Dad, seizing him by the shoulders. "You take pictures. Take all the pictures."

"Do you have a camera?" said the man.

"No, you do," said Dad. "It's that big thing with a lens around your neck."

"No, Dad, he's expecting you to give him your camera," said Nat. "He thinks you want him to take a picture of us, on your camera, obviously."

"I have a better idea," said Dad, as he heard the clip-clopping of a horse-drawn carriage. "You stand there with your big camera."

"Please?" said the man, confused. "I am Henrik Henriksonn, from Norway. I like to take the pictures of the pretty churches."

"Yes we know, take loads," said Dad. "Fill your church-loving Norwegian boots, just make sure you get lots of pictures of the bride too."

"Oh, OK," said the man, unsure.

"And hold your big camera up," said Dad, "make sure the bride sees you with it."

"It's a custom in England," said Nat, desperately. "If anyone asks, say you're the wedding photographer. It's for good luck."

"I'm not the wedding photographer, I am Henrik Henriksonn a tourist from Norway and I am here to take the photos of the pretty—"

"Yes, we know," said Nat, "but look, if you take some pictures you can have um…" She tried to think of something to offer him. "Cake! Do you like cake?"

"I don't like cake. So I say goodbye to you now."

The man started to move away, but Darius grabbed his sleeve.

"If you take lots of pictures for us," he said, "the vicar will show you bits of the church no one ever sees. Secret church stuff."

"This is good," said the man, smiling. "I go home with best church pictures. I am in a photography club."

"That's interesting, great," said Nat. "I'm pleased for you. "Have you got a big flash on that thing?"

"Peter Petersonn always wins competitions with his stupid church pictures at night. Big deal, night it is boring."

"Mmm, even more interesting," said Nat. "Anyway, just point your camera at the bride a lot, OK?"

"But then I will be taking the secret church photos?"

"Promise," said Nat and Darius, fibbing in unison.

Henrik Henriksonn pottered off to take pictures of the bride.

"That was easy," said Dad cheerfully. "Now, I need to go and do some ushering. Nat, get inside and get playing. This is definitely the right church this time. And take your coat off."

Nat took a deep breath and threw off her jacket to reveal the full glory/horror of the Perfect Fairy Princess Bridesmaid outfit. Her pink wings shimmered in the morning sun.

"Darius, you massive chimp," she said, "help me out. As I walk in, everyone's gonna want pictures of this stupid dress. I want as few pictures of me as possible, OK?"

"I'll distract them, don't worry," he said with an evil grin.

"Right, I'm going in, cover me."

She skipped quickly through the throng of wedding guests, who all *ooohed* and *aaaahed* at the pretty little fairy princess. But just as the guests were reaching for their cameras and phones, a huge, farty trumpety sound ripped through the air.

Whoa, you're gonna injure yourself doing that, thought Nat.

But Darius was blowing a real trumpet. Well, a flugelhorn. It was Uncle Spiro's flugelhorn, the one he used at the circus. It made a sound like a flatulent warthog that's spent a week eating baked-bean-and-cabbage sandwiches.

No one wanted to look at the fairy princess; they were all too busy looking out for wiffy warthogs.

Nat dashed up the church steps where the organist was waiting for her.

"You're just in time," he said. "I've got the music ready. Do you need to warm up?"

"No, I've played it once already this morning," said Nat, shuddering.

The flugelhorn stopped with a kind of strangled note and Nat guessed someone was wrestling it off Darius. Or possibly inserting it up his nostril.

Nat played the first few breathy chords on the organ. It sounded deep and rich and lovely. She craned her neck over the balcony to see the altar where Hiram, in a beautiful white silk suit, was waiting nervously.

That reminded her of Oswald's wedding to come in under an hour and for the zillionth time she checked her pocket for the pair of special, irreplaceable wedding rings.

They weren't there.

CHAPTER TWENTY-ONE

· · · ·

NAT HIT A HORRIBLE CHORD IN PANIC.

"You said you'd warmed up," said the organist, holding his hands over his ears.

"It's a new version," snapped Nat, "it's a remix."

She went back to the tune, as the crowd inside the church turned, excited, to welcome the arrival of the bride.

Her panic made her fingers hit a lot of the wrong notes, but she didn't care.

She pounded the keyboard with her tiny fists

in frustration.

"This is awful," said the organist, trying to drag her away.

"You're telling me it's awful," shouted Nat. "I've got another wedding in a bit and if I don't find these rings, Oswald Bagley will kill me."

The organist stopped dead in his tracks.

"Oswald Bagley?"

"Oh, have you heard of him?"

The organist shuddered. "You'll have to emigrate," he said. Yeah, you've heard of him, thought Nat, hitting more dodgy notes. "I know I put the rings on the table by the door," she said, thinking hard as she pounded tunelessly away at the organ, which shrieked and howled in protest. "And I thought I picked them up but…"

Suddenly she knew where they were! The rings were still on the side table by the front door… where Annie Chicken slammed down the bouquet. Tiffannee must have scooped up the rings and the flowers together!

Tiffannee was walking up the aisle.

"Look in her flowers, look in her flowers," she told the organist. "Can you see anything?"

The organist put on his gasses and squinted down at the bride. Tiffannee had stopped in the middle of the church, trying to see why the heck Nat was making such a horrible racket.

"Yes! There's something glinting in the blooms," he said.

"Great," said Nat, breathing a sigh of relief and actually playing the right notes at last. "I'm saved."

"Just make sure you catch the bouquet..." said the organist. "I knew someone who upset Oswald Bagley once. He had to move to *Wolverhampton*."

"Poor man," said Nat, playing rather well.

The tune ended and Nat hopped off the stool.

"You're up," she said, "they need me up the front end now."

"Good luck!" said the organist as Nat skittered

down the steps and ran to join Tiffannee, Hiram and the two remaining evil bridesmaids.

As she trotted down the aisle she looked at all the relatives and butterflies took off in her stomach. There were SO MANY family members here. So many people to watch everything go wrong. If it did. When it did.

"Something's bound to go wrong," she heard a voice say and for a second she thought she might have said it herself, out loud. But then she realised it was just Bad News Nan.

Bad News Nan, in her swamp thing outfit, was sitting next to a thin old lady, her sister Nelly who was Tiffannee's gran. Both women were wearing gigantic hats that were locked together in what looked like alien mortal combat. Though Bad News Nan's hat was winning, thought Nat.

"I've never known a wedding where there hasn't been a disaster," droned Bad News Nan.

"Me too," sniffed Nelly, not to be out Bad-Newsed.

"But I get invited to more weddings than you," said Bad News Nan, "because a lot of people say you're a bad omen. Like a big black cloud of gloom, people say. Not me, of course, I don't say that, I just think you're unlucky."

Nelly pursed her lips and shuffled away from her sister, which was hard, as Bad News Nan's outfit just sort of flowed over her.

At the business end of the church, by the vicar, Hiram's best man, another American, known as Mike J Stenkowitz Jr, was holding up a laptop, and frowning.

"Where's Daddy?" asked Tiffannee, looking like she might cry. "He's supposed to be online. He has to give me away. That's the rule. I want my dad."

"Sorry, baby," said Hiram, "looks like he couldn't make it."

Nat watched Tiffannee's perfect face crumble. She felt awful for her. Nat looked over at her own daft Dad, sitting in the front row, reading the massive wedding planner, muttering to himself and sweating nervously. A huge wave of affection washed over her. She couldn't imagine getting married, but she knew that if she ever did she couldn't imagine it without him.

The big idiot.

Dad looked up and saw her. He gave his usual Dad lopsided grin and Nat thought she might actually cry.

"Look at little miss perfect fairy," hissed horrid Daisy Wetwipe to Tilly Saddle. "Now she's pretending to cry."

I'm so gonna get you today, vowed Nat, silently furious. *You just wait.*

The vicar had just started to say a few words of welcome when the church doors flew open and a man's voice rang out:

"STOP THE WEDDING!"

There was a pause. Everyone in church held their breath.

"It'll be something terrible," came a voice

from the crowd. "Ooooh, it's a complete disaster, I said it would be."

It was Bad News Nan's voice, obvs.

But she was wrong. It wasn't bad news at all. In fact it was brilliant news.

"Daddy!" yelled Tiffannee and ran the length of the church to throw her arms around her father. They had a massive hug and the whole church exploded with applause.

"I wasn't gonna let my little girl get married without me," said Raymonde.

Nat looked at her dad. Big fat tears were welling up in his eyes.

Oh stoppit, thought Nat, dabbing her own.

She looked at her watch. Eek they were running late. *Hurry up*, she thought, *I've got another wedding to go to.*

But no one was in a hurry and the whole church was weeping now.

"Who are those men in dark suits and

sunglasses, Daddy?" said Tiffannee, looking over her dad's shoulder.

"Oh they're just a couple of FBI agents, making sure I go back to the States, you know, 'cos of that tiny oil spill thing. They said I could come as long as they get an invite to the party." Nat noticed Tiffannee cringe.

"Shush Dad," said the bride, "don't tell everyone."

"People might just notice these two enormous men, love," said Raymonde.

It ISN'T just my dad who's loopy and embarrassing then, thought Nat. *Interesting…*

Raymonde hugged his mum, Granny Nelly, who spat on her hanky and wiped something off his cheek.

"Are they feeding you alright in that prison?" said Granny Nelly.

"Mum – I'm not in prison yet," said Raymonde, "and can you keep your voice down."

You know, thought Nat, *I bet there's cave paintings of our family embarrassing each other during woolly mammoth hunts.*

Soon – though not soon enough for nervous Nat, who was aware that the Bagley wedding was due to start any minute – the ceremony got underway. And everything else went according to plan, which Nat found hard to believe.

Even though Nat was obsessed by the ticking of the wedding clock, she had to admit the actual moment Tiffannee and Hiram got married was...

Flipping lovely.

If a bit soppy.

Finally the deed was done. Everyone trooped outside to wait for the newly-weds.

Next would be that magic moment when the bride throws away her bouquet. The bouquet with the Bagley rings! Nat heard Tilly Saddle say: "That bouquet is *mine*. I've been going out with Gary Axminster for three years, and it's about time he proposed."

We'll see about that, thought Nat, grimly. She

grabbed Darius and whispered something in his ear.

Then she said: "Do you EVER wash your ears? I could make a candle with all that wax."

Tiffannee and Hiram, man and wife, finally emerged into bright sunlight and people threw confetti, despite the big signs saying PLEASE DON'T THROW CONFETTI.

Or it might be because Darius had painted over the word DON'T in white paint.

Trapped Norwegian tourist, Henrik Henriksonn, was right in the thick of it, still taking pictures. He looked a bit confused, but seemed to be doing a good job.

Tiffannee stood at the top of the steps and prepared to throw her flowers to the waiting crowd. Tilly Saddle spat on her hands and crouched, ready to leap. But Nat had other ideas.

As soon as the bouquet was tossed in the air, Darius made a cup for his hands, which Nat stood on. He threw her upwards. Darius was small but surprisingly strong, and Nat was skinny and light.

She leapt up like a salmon in a hot pond. She sailed over everyone's heads and grabbed the flying flowers. The wings might even have helped.

YESSSSS! she thought, seeing the two rings in the flowers.

Then she realised how high she was.

NOOOO, she thought.

Splat.

She landed.

On poor Henrik Henriksonn.

"I've broken everything in my body," she wailed.

"You have broken ME," said the squished tourist. "Can I go now?"

"No," said Nat and Darius in unison.

"Gimmee that," said Tilly Saddle, grabbing at the bouquet. "It's MINE."

There were murmurs of "shame" and "rude" and "big bully" from the crowd.

Tilly forced a big fake smile. "We're only playing!" she said, picking Nat up and dusting her down and straightening her dented wings.

"Bridesmaid banter, that's right, isn't it, *bum 'ole*?"

Nat smiled a fake smile back – and stamped her foot down hard on Tilly's toes. And Nat was wearing her big heavy black boots.

Tilly went red in the face and cross-eyed with pain.

"Banter THAT," said Nat, grabbing the rings and running. She gave Tiffannee a peck on the cheek. "See you at the marquée!" said Nat.

"Where are you going?" asked Tiffannee, looking confused.

"Love you, must dash," shouted Nat over her shoulder, "I need to, er, I need to, um…"

She couldn't think of an excuse for dashing

off so quickly.

"SHE NEEDS A POO!" shouted Darius, running after her.

CHAPTER TWENTY-TWO

• • • •

"WHAT? THAT WAS A GREAT EXCUSE," SAID Darius in the back of the van, as they sped to the next wedding. "Stop... ow! Stop pinching, you're breaking the skin now."

Oswald's wedding ceremony was taking place outdoors, in the rose garden of the local park. By the time they got there, Nat had zipped up her black jacket over her fairy princess outfit and was looking less utterly lame.

"I got the rings, did you remember your thing?" she said to Darius, trying to keep a straight face and failing totally.

He held up his cuff, still locked on to his wrist. It jangled.

Nat could tell the Bagleys were already at the wedding because the roads around the park were blocked by an extraordinary selection of cars, vans and trucks.

A few, a very few, were modern and shiny. Most were not. There were battered pick-ups; old convertibles with silver sticky tape holding down the fabric roofs; big, dented estate cars with thick heavy tyres and cracked windscreens. There were old delivery vans and horseboxes and camper vans even tattier than the Atomic Dustbin.

They had to park miles away. "Run," said Nat, as the three of them jogged to the park. They made it inside with only a few minutes to spare.

Merlin was already there, under a black awning, next to a bubbling cauldron.

And also already there were:

THE BAGLEY CLAN.

If Nat had ever done her history homework, she might have known that today was the anniversary of the battle of Scrotalanium, as the town used to be called in Roman times.

Dad, who fancied himself as a bit of a local historian, DID know, although not as much as he pretended to. He whispered:

"It was right here, where we're standing. The roman legion under Squintus Maximus were faced by the wildest and most savage barbarians in the whole Empire," he said.

He looked around at the bunch of Bagleys, who were staring at them.

"It must have felt a bit like this," said Dad.

A roar went up from the wild wedding guests.

"Crikey, it's happening again," said cowardly Dad "let's go. It didn't end well for Maximus. He was called Minimus afterwards."

But Darius just ran into the crowd, where he was tossed from cousin to auntie to uncle to cousin again like a volleyball.

"They're FRIENDLY barbarians, Dad, we'll be fine," said Nat, stepping forward with a smile and getting swallowed up. She was petted and patted and passed around until she found herself next to Fiona and Merlin.

"Morning!" said Nat, who had decided the day was SO bonkers she might as well try to enjoy herself. "Nice day for a wedding, what's in the cauldron? Breakfast?"

"Bats, rats, toads, weasels and some secret herbs and spices," said Fiona, kissing Nat. "But it'll probably taste like chicken. Have you got...?"

Nat produced the rings and Darius appeared, jangling his cuffs.

"Phew," said Fiona.

"Where is Oswald?" intoned Merlin the dry-cleaner.

As if to reply, Oswald stepped out of the bushes. He stood straight and tall and proud. He was clad all in black leather, and his beard was plaited in two, like a Viking. The only colour on him was his face, which was painted with two bright blue stripes across his cheeks, and on his beard, where two tiny flames flickered and smoked from the ends.

"He's quite handsome, in a totally terrifying way," said Nat, "but I might only be saying that 'cos those fumes from the cauldron are making me feel odd."

"He's lush," said Fiona, looking at him with an expression Nat recognised as GROWN UP.

Ew, thought Nat, *public display of*

affection coming, ew ew ew.

The ceremony began and although it was quite odd, Nat didn't think it was much odder than the one in the church. As far as she could tell, they were both just old men in robes banging on about something or other in deep booming voices.

The couple lit candles and drank some of the disgusting brew, and Fiona said something about Oswald being the other half of her, which Nat thought sounded revolting.

Then the time came for Oswald to say his bit.

Oooh, I'm finally gonna hear Oswald speak, thought Nat, *can't wait.*

But, just then, the mounting fumes from the cauldron caught the back of her throat and she started coughing, and couldn't stop. She bent double as tears fell, streaming, down her face and she gasped for air.

Dad rushed over. "She's choking!" he said, thumping her back and squeezing her ribs while she kept trying to fight him off. "My little girl's choking, give her air, never mind all the wizardry..."

By the time she'd recovered, though, the ceremony had moved on and she'd missed Oswald's big moment.

"Who bears the rings?" said Merlin Tolpuddle gravely.

"That would be me," said Nat, handing them over. Merlin put the rings on the couple. The Bagley clan made a kind of *ooooh* noise.

"Who bears the cuffs of togetherness?" said Merlin. No one moved. Merlin prodded Darius with his staff.

"Is that me?" said Darius, and stepped forward, jangling his handcuffs. Oswald produced the key with a wide smile.

"I know where that's been," said Darius, grumpily.

"And now will the Maid of Horror step forward?" said Merlin.

Nat did as she was instructed. She felt like

she was in a film; it was all quite fun. Merlin, the shaman of the dirty shirts, took her arm and placed it over the bubbling cauldron.

"And will the Prince of Misrule step forward to join her?"

Merlin took Darius's arm too and made them hold hands.

Urgh, less fun, thought Nat.

"Now, I join the two families together," said Merlin, holding the handcuffs.

"I'm not really family," began Nat.

But Fiona shushed her. "You're the closest thing I've got to a little sister," she said, gently.

"Ahh, that's so nice," said Nat, eyes filling with tears again.

What is it with weddings and blubbing? she thought. *Get a grip, Nat.*

Then Merlin placed the other cuff around her wrist.

"Hold it right there, beardy," she said.

"Don't worry, it's just for a minute," said Fiona.

"It's part of the wedding binding ceremony."

CLUNK went the heavy iron cuff.

And Nat was joined…

To Darius Bagley.

Merlin did a bit more mumbo jumbo then at last said: "Release the Maid of Horror and the Prince of Misrule."

Oswald passed the key towards Merlin. The shaman of the dirty collars couldn't quite reach, so ever-helpful Dad took the key…

And dropped it RIGHT IN THE CAULDRON.

"Ooops, butterfingers!" said Dad.

Nat was totally chained to Darius.

"Get it out," said Nat, glaring at Dad, "get that key out, right now."

"We cannot touch the cauldron until it is cooled," said Merlin. "It is forbidden. It is taboo." He looked down at the bubbling goo. "Also it's flipping hot and I'll get scalded," he muttered under his breath.

Nat looked at her watch. It was on the side

attached to Darius and she nearly dragged him into the steaming pot.

"Watch out," he said.

"We've gotta get to Tiffannee's reception in twenty minutes," Nat hissed at Darius, panic rising in her voice. Then she yelled at Merlin: "Oi, Dumbledore, will it be cool in ten minutes?"

"Ten minutes? You'll be lucky. Give it a couple of hours, more like," said Merlin, who wasn't sounding very wizard-like any more, "or possibly not till tomorrow, to be on the safe side."

"Where's the spare key?" Nat asked Fiona hopefully, trying to pull her hand out of the old cuffs.

"There isn't a spare key," said Fiona, "and stop wriggling, you'll never get out of them without a key. Even Fingers Bagley never got out of those cuffs. They're the best ever made. You'll just have a wait a while, together. You don't mind, do you? Seeing as you're such good friends. It's all part of the magic of weddings."

"When today is over, Dad..." growled Nat, dangerously.

Merlin turned to Fiona and Oswald. "I have just one more duty to perform," he said, reaching into his robe. He pulled out a business card and handed it over to them.

"You get two-for-one dry-cleaning for the first three months of your marriage. All part of the service."

He raised his staff and shouted:

"That's it – they're married!" A great cheer went up.

"I am available for other ceremonies," Merlin went on, even though no one could hear him over the great Bagley cheering, "christenings, funerals and children's parties too."

"Yay and woop for flipping weddings" said Nat wearily, "and extra cheering for bridesmaid-ing."

She felt her hand get lifted up towards Darius's

face. She yanked her cuff, sharply.

"Ow, you almost pulled my nose off," said Darius.

"Stop picking it then," she said crossly.

Then she realised what else he would do with his hands over A WHOLE DAY.

"AAAARRGH!" she yelled. "Get them off now!" but no one in the cheering crowd heard her scream.

CHAPTER TWENTY-THREE

. . . .

"Any ideas?" said Nat.

Nat and Darius were sat facing each other across the little camping table in the back of Dad's van, the cuffs lying on the table between them.

"Power tools," said Darius.

"Any other ideas?" said Nat. She knew how rubbish Dad's DIY skills were.

They had been home to pick up the big bowls of Dad's wedding stew which were now clanging around in the back of the van. They were now off to serve the stew at Tiffannee's perfect olde English summer wedding marquée, formerly known as Spiro's Super Circus.

Then they would just have enough time to dash to the Castle Country Club, where Penny and Mr Posnitch were making a posh lunch.

Dad's phone bonged.

"That's a text," he said passing his phone back. "Can you look for me, I'm driving."

Nat leaned over to grab the phone, pulling Darius with her. His face hit the table with a smack.

"Thanks," Darius said, "I've been trying to get that tooth out for ages."

"Sorry, I forgot," said Nat, giving him another yank for luck.

"Oh heck, it's from Mum," said Nat, reading the text. "She got an earlier flight!"

"HHHNNNNG," said Dad.

"She's heading to the the Castle Country Club," shouted Nat, "she's expecting it to be

Tiffannee's wedding, Dad!"

The van swerved and Dad said some rude words.

"I hadn't QUITE told your mum the full story," said Dad, "I was going to say we found this new venue in a field in an old circus and it was definitely way better than the country club, but then I thought that might make her a bit completely furious so I had a better plan which was to hope Mum's meetings ran over and she missed the wedding altogether."

"That's not a plan, Dad," said Nat, appalled.

"It's not a GOOD plan, I agree," said Dad, "but it was a plan."

Nat put her head in her hands.

"I had a back-up plan too," said Dad.

Hope flared up in Nat briefly, like so many times before.

"That plan was to pray she saw the funny side."

Nat's hope was immediately squished, like so

many times before.

"It sometimes takes a while to see the funny side," said Dad, "but you can usually see it eventually."

Nat glared at Dad.

"I can see you glaring in the rear view mirror," said Dad, "and it's putting me off driving. Look, I'll call your mum when we get to the circus – I mean olde worlde perfect English wedding marquée – and tell her to come there instead. She'll probably think I did all the right things anyway."

"Like she always does you mean?" said Nat.

"Well, um…" said Dad, uncomfortably.

Darius grinned. Eventually Nat joined him. "You're right about one thing, Dad," said Nat.

"Am I?" said Dad, who didn't hear that often.

"Yeah. I AM starting to see the funny side."

The van stopped at some traffic lights, and the useless engine cut out. All three of them suddenly noticed a loud slurping sound coming from the back.

Nat and Dad instinctively looked at Darius.

"It's not me," said Darius.

"Where's the dog?" Nat said suddenly. "He's usually licking Darius 'cos he's the most tasty thing in the van to— uh oh."

She dived into the back, dragging Darius with her, who clanged his face on a pan.

"Forgot again, sorry," she yelled. Then she saw the mutt. He was lying on his back with a very happy look on his doggy face.

A doggy face covered in gravy.

Well, stew.

Dad stew.

"HE'S EATEN THE STEW!" yelled Nat, "Dad, the dog's munched Tiffannee's wedding lunch."

"He'll be OK, it was just meat and potatoes," said Dad starting the van again.

"Never mind THE DOG," shouted Nat. "Listen to what I said. I said he's EATEN

Tiffannee's WEDDING LUNCH!"

"All of it?" squeaked Dad nervously.

"Dunno," said Nat as she and Darius went through the pots and cartons of food. The crafty hound had started munching right at the back so they hadn't seen the havoc he'd caused until too late. Pot after pot and carton after carton had been sniffed, investigated, licked, tasted...

...and gobbled right up.

Only a few pots remained undisturbed.

"There's about half left," said Nat, "but that's got dog hairs in."

"Fish 'em out," said Dad. "There's nothing poisonous about dog hair."

"Dad, we can't serve wedding guests half a plate of hairy stew," said Nat. "I mean, it's not like everything else today has gone tickety-boo. Tiffannee's sitting in a field in a Bagley circus tent with two out of six bridesmaids and a wedding photographer who's a kidnapped Norwegian tourist, and half the FBI. The disco's just Darius with an iPod and the band is you and Miss Hunny on a ukulele. The least we could do is give them some proper food, not furry dog-slobber."

She wanted to bang her head on the little table. Instead, she yanked her arm and clanged Darius off a portable stove.

"If you're gonna look on the dark side all the time…" said Dad.

"Right, that's it!" Nat dashed forward to throttle her dad.

"Glark," said Darius, who was dragged behind her and was now wedged between two large cast iron pans.

Fortunately for Dad that meant Nat was pulled up short before she could get her fingers around his neck.

"The cake!" yelled Dad. "Tell me that the cake's OK."

In the panic over the slurped stew, Nat had forgotten about the cake. It was in the back under a large protective sheet.

"I'm too scared to look," she said. Darius wasn't. He whipped off the cover to reveal…

A perfect, three-tiered, beautiful white wedding cake.

"It's fine, Dad," said Nat with a huge sigh of relief.

"See? Maybe our luck's changed," he said, ramming on the brakes to avoid Merlin Tolpuddle's dry-cleaning van which had just pulled out in front of him without looking.

"That was close," said Dad, honking the horn and wagging a warning finger at the shaman. "Everyone all right in the back?"

There was a silence.

"Not really," said Darius.

Dad looked in the rear view mirror.

Nat was sitting with a totally stunned expression on her face.

And the top tier of the wedding cake…

Squished on her head.

CHAPTER TWENTY-FOUR

· · · ·

THE CAKE WAS IN A TERRIBLE MESS.

Nat's hair was in a terrible mess.

And Dad was terribly lost.

"TIFFANNEE'S WEDDING IS TURNING INTO A TERRIBLE MESS," wailed Nat, as Dad pulled up at a garage so Nat could get cleaned up and he could get directions.

She was far too miserable to even help as Dad wiped several kilos of cake off her with some garage-bought wet wipes. Darius helped by eating a lot of it.

The top of the cake was smooshed to smithereens, but Darius reckoned the rest of it could be saved.

"Too late, the wedding is doomed anyway," said Nat, "and I'm going to look totally rubbish in front of all our relatives. Plus, I feel bad for Tiffannee. I know it's all Dad's fault but I feel a teeny bit responsible."

"We can get away with it. We just need to give the cake a different shape," said Darius, looking thoughtful. "Then no one will know the top's missing."

"Oh that's a great help," snapped Nat. "Who's gonna do that? You'd need to be the greatest sculptor in the word to turn this cake into anything…"

Her voice trailed off. Her eyes lit up.

She knew just the man for the job.

"Please be in, please be in," said Nat as she waited at Uncle Ernie's front door.

Darius pressed the doorbell again. Uncle Ernie had changed the normally happy doorbell song to one that went:

"*I don't know why you've come, no one likes me...*"

Eventually Uncle Ernie opened the door. He was cuddling Buster, his big, fluffy rescue dog. He started to smile at Nat, and then remembered her last visit.

"What now?" he said. "Have you remembered someone else who doesn't like me?"

He looked at Darius, still attached to Nat and raised his eyebrows. "Long story, no time," said Nat. Then she took a deep breath and began. "Uncle Ernie, Tiffannee made a terrible mistake and she's really sorry. She was being silly because... well, I think getting married makes people go a bit odd, to tell you the truth. I've no idea why."

"So?"

"So *please* come to the wedding. It won't be

the same without you," said Nat, trying to stand somewhere so as to not get the full benefit of the cabbagey smell. "Families have to be together at weddings. That's what they're for."

"And Buster?"

"He's family too," said Nat. "Will you come?"

Uncle Ernie smiled his wonky smile. "I'll get my coat," he said.

"And while you're at it, bring your modelling tools," Nat shouted after him, looking nervously up at the sky as a few fat drops of rain fell and dark clouds began to gather overhead.

By the time they reached the wedding tent, the sky was looking heavy and ominous, as if something terrible was going to happen soon. But Nat didn't have time to think about that – she was too busy trying to deal with all the terrible things that were happening right now.

Nat knew all the guests would be getting hungry and cranky. There was no time to lose.

While Uncle Ernie furiously remodelled the stricken cake, Dad started unloading what was left of the hairy, doggy stew into the cooking caravans.

Nat spent a terrible few minutes trying to untangle herself from her cool black clothes to reveal her horrid fairy outfit. This was not easy, attached to Darius. At one point, his revolting head popped up from under her top and she shrieked in fright.

Finally it was done and they went to find Tiffannee.

They found her in the tent with Hiram, her dad and the bridesmaids. All the guests were crowded inside, sitting at long trestle tables, waiting for their lunch.

The loudest voice belonged, of course, to Bad News Nan, who was STARVING.

"I've decided not to let my son and grandaughter organise my funeral," she droned to some poor relatives who couldn't get away, "everyone would be so hungry they'd end up eating me."

"What a DISGUSTING thought," said Grandma Nelly.

"What's wrong with eating me?" said Bad News Nan.

"I like lean meat," snapped Grandma Nelly, "if you get my drift."

"Well I don't imagine *you'd* make good eating," said Bad News Nan, "all stringy and sour's what I say. Gristle, I call it.""

"Will you stop talking about eating my mum?" snapped Raymonde, as the FBI men chuckled nearby.

"We could put her in a pie," said Bad News Nan.

Nat was distracted from that mad conversation by the bride, who ran down to greet her. "Where have you been?" said Tiffannee. "And why are you holding that boy's hand?"

Nat had bundled all her black clothes into a ball and covered the cuffs with them. It worked as a disguise but looked like she was holding hands with Darius.

Now Nat saw that Tiffannee was looking a little cross.

"And will you tell this photographer to leave me alone for a minute?"

Henrik Henriksonn was still there, taking pictures. "Can I go home now?" he said.

"No," said Nat firmly. "More pictures, but of other people."

She chased him away, taking Darius with her, which slowed things up a lot. When she returned she saw Daisy Wetwipe whispering in Tiffannee's ear. By the wrinkled-up nose of the chief bridesmaid, Nat guessed she was being all moany about the marquée.

Uh oh, she thought, I knew it. Not so fast, you.

She turned to Tiffannee and put on her most winning smile. "Do you know this marquée used to belong to Henry the eighth?" she said.

"Gee honey, you hear that? said Hiram, who like all Americans was a sucker for a bit of history, even history that was TOTALLY MADE UP, "and Daisy here was just saying it looked like a ratty old big top from a manky circus."

Did she indeed? thought Nat. OK then, two can play at that game. "She's not had much education," said Nat, "so I don't blame her for her mistake."

"Now Nat…" said Tiffannee, who looked a bit rattled by Daisy's constant moaning, but was trying her best to stay calm, "where's lunch? There's only so much conversation about cooking each other I can listen to. I think it means people are peckish."

Nat couldn't think what to say.

"Lunch is late. Marcel wants perfection," said Darius.

"Marcel?" said Hiram.

"Perfection?" said Tiffannee.

"Rot," muttered Daisy.

"It's another surprise," said Nat.

"Another one?" said Tiffannee, through slightly gritted teeth. "Gee, Nat, I wonder how many more of your surprises I can stand."

"Marcel is a great French chef," said Nat, thinking on her feet, "he loves perfection but he can't speak English so don't even think about talking to him."

"French?" sneered Daisy Wetwipe, "a French chef doing the food at a perfect ENGLISH wedding? Oh dear."

"It's very English food," snapped Nat.

"It's so English he's not allowed to cook it in France," said Darius.

"Um, OK," said Tiffannee. "And what's Marcel made for lunch? You said it was going to be amazing."

"Did I say amazing?" said Nat, nervously. "I thought I said surprising."

"Nah, you probably said hairy," said Darius,

followed by: "ow."

"I said interesting," said Nat, "yes, let's go with interesting."

"Yes but what IS for lunch?" said Tiffannee.

"Here it comes now," said Nat, as Dad hurried in with big hot steaming bowls. "Everyone take your seats, lunch is served!"

The bridal party seated themselves at the top table as Dad served up the stew, making sure they got theirs first. Tiffannee and Hiram were in the middle, with Tiffannee's dad and of course the FBI agents on one side. Hiram's best man and Daisy sat together on the other. But there was no Tilly Saddle.

"That's right, Nat," said Daisy, "yet another bridesmaid's been got rid of. She's getting her toes X-rayed for some reason."

Nat and Darius tried to look innocent. There was a clap of thunder overhead.

"I hope there's lots, I'm starving," said Tiffannee's dad, "and my FBI agents eat like horses."

Dad went and got the rest of the stew and placed the bowls in the middle of the rest of the tables.

"That's the lot," said Dad. "Tuck in!"

The guests looked at the bowls, did a quick head count, and made a calculation as to how much there was each.

Those who were faster at maths grabbed a ladle and spooned the stew out on to their plates, pronto.

"It's very filling, don't go mad," said Dad nervously.

"This isn't EXACTLY what I expected," said Tiffannee. She looked at Nat. "And WHY are you two still holding hands?"

"Wedding fever," said Nat.

"That is SO sweet," said Hiram's best man, "what's your name, you little scamp?"

"Professor Willy Wetfartz," said Darius.

Dad bustled over with another half a bowl of

stew he'd wrestled off Bad News Nan.

"Eat up," he said, "this is a once in a life time dish."

"Is this meat?" said Daisy, looking at her food, "only I'm thinking seriously about becoming a vegetarian. Good weddings have vegetarian options."

"Marcel says his vegetarian option is to take the bits of meat out," said Nat.

Daisy scowled but Tiffannee suddenly burst out laughing. "Oh come on, lighten up," she said to Daisy. "You can't argue with a master chef like Marcel. You can always fill up on cake later."

A few minutes later, Dad called Nat over to a quiet bit of the tent. Obviously she had to drag Darius with her, which annoyed him as he hadn't finished his stew.

"Have you seen the comedy waiters?" said Dad.

"The what?"

"I booked this hilarious group for the

wedding," said Dad. "They're amazing. They start by being waiters, but then they get everything wrong and the guests think it's real."

"Dad, it's all going wrong anyway," said Nat crossly, "you don't have to pay for that, you spanner."

"It's part of their act. They get into arguments with the guests, drop stuff everywhere and pretend to fight each other. It's hilarious."

"No, that's embarrassing and lame."

"Then at the end they sing wedding songs. It's brilliant!"

"OK, whatevs, but where are they then?"

Dad sighed. "Dunno. Sometimes I don't think organising stuff is my very strongest skill. I remember booking them for the Castle Country Club and then... oh hang on." He slapped his forehead, remembering. "I forgot to tell them about the change of venue... They'll be round there."

Nat looked at her watch, nearly pulling

Darius's arm out of its socket. "We should be there too, by now," she said, hopping about in panic. "Fiona and Oswald will wonder where we are. I just hope their lunch is less of a dog's dinner than this one."

"That's a good joke," said Dad, "because 'dogs dinner' means 'a total mess' AND lunch was, in fact, dinner for the dog."

"I'm not finding any of this funny, Dad," said Nat, "let's see if Uncle Ernie's got the cake ready." They dashed through a flap at the back of the big top, ducking against the steady rain, and ran to the fortune teller's tent, where Uncle Ernie was repairing the cake.

"It's not ready, go away," shouted Uncle Ernie, from the gloom, "and don't look, you'll spoil the surprise."

"Is the cake made of cabbage?" said Darius, wrinkling his nose at the smell. Nat yanked him away and they dashed back towards the big top.

"We HAVE to go, Dad," yelled Nat.

"OK but we'll have to stall the guests till we get back and do the cake," said Dad, "we need some entertainment."

"NONE of our relatives are entertaining, Dad," said Nat, "including you, by the way."

"But mine are," said Darius, stopping dead.

"Aren't they all over at Oswald and Fiona's wedding?" said Nat.

"Nah," said Darius, "loads of people hate weddings."

"I know how they feel," said stressed-out Nat, who was getting soaked.

But Darius was already dragging her off towards another caravan,

"They might hate weddings," he said, banging on the door, "but they all love performing."

Five minutes later, Nat and Darius rushed back into the big top where it was clear the still-peckish guests were starting to grumble.

"This better work," Nat hissed.

"Get on with it," said Darius.

Nat took a deep breath. "LAYDEEEZ AND GENTLEMEN," she shouted, feeling like a complete wingnut as all her relatives stared at her. "I've got some awesome wedding day entertainment," she said. "For between courses."

"It's not your dad and his rotten ukulele is it?" shouted Granny Nelly, making everyone laugh. Nat went red.

"No it's not," she snapped, "it's actually good."

And then she squealed and ducked as a big explosion of flame went off overhead.

"Are you setting light to your farts again?" she shouted at Darius.

But it was just Cedric the fireater, leading the wedding-hating circus folk into the tent.

There were two scary-looking clowns, a one-legged acrobat, an old lady with a trained dog called Simon, a wheezy pensioner who did card tricks, a contortionist with a bad back and the fortune teller, glad of an excuse to leave her now-whiffy tent.

They're not the greatest circus performers ever, thought Nat, watching as they began, but they're still better than Dad.

"Gotta go, doing more surprises," Nat shouted at Tiffannee, who was looking a bit bewildered, "back soon."

Nat ran outside for the van, dragging Darius and grabbing Dad as she went.

The storm was really picking up. Rain was falling steadily now. They ran, trying to dodge the drops.

"And where do you think you're going?" said a voice they couldn't dodge.

CHAPTER TWENTY-FIVE

· · · ·

IT WAS BAD NEWS NAN. HOLDING A PLATE.

"Actually, I know where you're going. And I'm coming too," she said. "Now hurry up I'm getting wet."

"Do you know about the other wedding?" asked Dad, as they all piled into the van.

"I do. And I know there's better food at the Country Club too, so you can take me there now, thank you. I'm famished."

"How…?" said Dad. "I never said anything."

Bad News Nan sniffed and polished her

false teeth on her skirt. "Well, you never tell me anything. I'm kept in the dark, I am. It's why I have to read everyone's email and listen to their phone messages. It's not nice that you make me do that."

"Nan!" said Nat, shocked.

"And you've done some soft things, Ivor," said Bad News Nan, shaking her head, "but getting caught up with the Bagleys is about the softest. They're a properly bad lot." She rubbed the top of Darius's mucky head. "Except this one."

Darius snuggled into Bad News Nan's bosom. Even Nat couldn't yank him out.

"Whatever you do," intoned Bad News Nan in her usual VOICE OF DOOM, "don't upset them. You better make sure they have a good wedding."

"We're trying, Nan," said Nat, feeling like she was about to pass out with tiredness and stress. "We're ever so really trying."

Nat – back in black – wasn't sure she knew what a good Bagley wedding should look like, but as she entered the dining room of the Country Club, she saw what THIS Bagley wedding looked like.

Utter chaos.

There must have been over a hundred guests. And they were all having… A BALL. They were shouting and drinking and toasting and cheering. There was kissing, fighting, sleeping and arm wrestling.

"Oh good," said Darius, "they haven't got going yet."

Kids were running about the place, scampering under tables, jumping on and off laps, hanging off black curtains, yanking at black tablecloths, or knocking the black decorations off.

Every so often a harassed Bagley mother would chase one round the room before giving them, or the nearest random child, a wallop. Then the child would yell at the top of its voice, and then they'd get a cuddle and a boiled sweetie, and they'd be off again.

"All the kids look like you," said Nat, "the poor little things."

She saw Bad News Nan had already fought her way into the Bagley throng, and was gossiping with old Grammy Bagley. Bad News Nan took a silver flask from her handbag, drank from it and handed it to the other grandma. She grabbed it, took a great gulp, and emptied it.

Then Grammy Bagley took an even bigger flask from her purse and handed it to Bad News Nan.

I dunno what's worse, thought Nat, *them fighting or them being friends*. She could see her life filled with double grim nan doom. She was beginning to feel like she really was becoming a Bagley.

"Where did you dash off to?" said newly-wed PC Fiona Sweetly-Bagley, walking over to say hello. "Ohhhh, I get it," she said, looking at Darius and Nat holding hands, and giving them a wink. "Your secret is safe with me."

She giggled.

"You *know* why we're holding hands," said Nat. "It's your grandad's flipping handcuffs. Is that cauldron cool yet?"

"Never mind that," said Fiona. "Grandad's actually *here*. I've been dying for you to meet him. We haven't got a big family, but pretty much all the Sweetlys have come. They're at that table there, look."

Among the crowds of noisy, twitchy, shouty, singing, cheering Bagleys, there were two tables who were NOT having a good time.

One was full of youngish men and women with neat haircuts, sitting up very straight. Nat guessed, correctly, that they were Fiona's police buddies. They were trying to ignore the Bagleys. Which was pretty hard.

The other table was filled by a small group of stern-looking relatives, also pretending the room wasn't crammed with Oswald's huge and noisy family.

Fiona ushered Nat and Darius over to the table. A large, slim elderly man with eyes and nose like a hawk stared at the cuffs.

"I've missed you," he said, stroking the heavy iron things. "We had some good times together."

"I thought it was you," said another old man, appearing from behind Nat. He looked weather-beaten and tough, like one of the more successful pirates.

"We meet again, Fingers Bagley," said Fiona's grandad, standing up. The two men were nose to nose, with Nat and Darius squashed in between.

"I was never nicking that safe," said Fingers. "I was taking it to get it cleaned."

"Tell it to the judge," snarled Grandad Sweetly. "Oh wait, you *did*, and the judge didn't believe you either."

"I should strangle you with these," said Fingers Bagley, grabbing the cuffs and lifting them up, taking Nat and Darius with them.

"Try me any time," said the old policeman.

Fingers looked down at the dangling children. "Hello, Darius. Pleased to meet you, little miss," he said politely. "Welcome to our family."

Darius chuckled.

Oh heck, thought Nat.

The old bank robber set them down again and went back to his table.

"*Why are we waiting…*" sang the hungry Bagleys, bashing the tables with their knives and forks.

"These lot aren't as polite as Tiffannee's guests," said Nat, running towards the kitchens, Darius dragged behind her, bouncing off the tables. "I hope Penny and her dad have got the food ready," she said.

She was relieved to sniff delicious cooking smells from the kitchen. Inside there was almost as much chaos as there was outside. Mr Posnitch, covered in flour, sauces and a sprinkling of secret herbs and spices, was hitting himself on the head with a rolling pin. Penny, also covered in ingredients, was near tears.

Tears at a wedding, thought Nat. *What a surprise.*

"No, no, NO," Mr Posnitch was shouting, "there are NO currants in proper Sclutch Dumplings. Why did you put currents in the Sclutch Dumplings? You have to start all over again."

"No starting again!" said Nat firmly. "Just lots of getting it straight out into the dining room, as fast as possible."

"Nathalia, this is all terrible," moaned Mr Posnitch. "I am a professional, I am used to professional kitchen, but here, no. There is no equipment!"

Nat looked round. The Country Club kitchen was jammed with every possible utensil she could think of, from pans to lemon squeezers, from blenders and mixers to blow torches and bread makers.

"I am expected to cook my food without a

Gremki steamer, a sutch muddler or even a flump griddle. How is it possible?"

"It certainly smells yummy," said Nat, side-stepping the question neatly.

"You call it yummy, I say is *slop*," said Mr Posnitch. "Is fit only for pigs and wild beasts."

"That's perfect," said Darius cheerfully.

"Why are you picking Darius's nose?" said Penny.

"AAARGH!" shouted Nat, looking at her hand and realising what Darius was doing. "Stop it. Now."

Penny gave her dad a big hug. "Dad, it's all lovely, I promise. It tastes the way Mum would have made it."

Nat knew Penny didn't have a mum any more.

Mr Posnitch's eyes sparkled, damply.

Oh not you too, thought Nat.

He drew himself up to his full tiny height. "If it is good enough for Mariska Popitova Posnitch, it is good enough for a queen," said Mr Posnitch, "because that is what she was, a queen."

He began taking the black-coloured food out, proudly.

"Thanks for asking Dad to help," said Penny. "He hasn't enjoyed cooking for years, not since Mum…. This has really cheered him up."

Nat's lower lip trembled.

"It's OK, Penny," she sniffed. "I'm just glad to bring a bit of happiness into people's lives."

"It's made me so happy too," sobbed Penny. The girls fell wetly into each other's arms, tears flowing freely.

"Darius, is that your finger up my nose?" said Penny.

"I need a wee," said Darius.

"You can't have one!" said Nat, furiously, all tears forgotten.

"It's gonna run down my leg," he said.

"I don't care, just keep your hands where I can see them," said Nat. Darius crossed and uncrossed his legs.

Dad appeared in the doorway. "You gotta see this…" he said. The three children rushed out into the dining room. Mr Posnitch was being chucked about over the heads of the Bagleys like a floury volleyball.

"Put my dad down, you monsters!" yelled Penny.

CHAPTER TWENTY-SIX

. . . .

"PLEASE DON'T HURT HIM," SOBBED PENNY. "I'm sorry about the sultanas in the dumplings, I didn't know…"

She rushed forward to rescue him, but Dad stopped her. He was laughing. "They're not hurting him," he said smiling. "They're saying thank you for the delicious food. They think he's wonderful!"

Bounce bounce bounce went Mr Posnitch.

"Posnitch, Posnitch," chanted the Bagleys.

"It's just like when he scored the winning goal

in the cup final!" said Penny, sounding super-proud. "Shame it was an own goal, and it was the other team who were thanking him, but still…"

The meal was a great success.

Once again, Nat and Dad had avoided upsetting Oswald. Better yet, Nat managed to get some of Mr Posnitch's delicious food, which was fortunate as she'd (deliberately) missed out on Tiffannee's doggy stew earlier and was ravenous.

The only difficulty was trying to eat while being attached to Darius. She had to time it or he'd end up with lunch all over his face. Which he did most days anyway, so actually she wasn't that bothered. In fact…

Splat! went yet another spoonful of apple pie and custard, up his nose. *Tee hee*, thought Nat, *this is the best part of the day so far*.

"You gotta get the key to the cuffs," said custard-nosed Darius, even twitchier than normal, "or I'm gonna burst, and if I burst who's gonna get splashed? You, that's who."

"Fiona! Where's Merlin and where's the key?" yelled Nat.

"He's been called away on an emergency," said Fiona. "There was an explosion at the tomato sauce bottling plant."

"Oh, I didn't realise he was a doctor," said Nat. "I thought he worked in the dry-cleaner's?"

"That's the emergency," said Fiona. "Four hundred shirts, ruined by ketchup. He'll be kept busy all day."

"All right, just gimme a hair pin," said Darius, through gritted teeth, "under the table so no one can see."

Fiona found one in her bag and Darius began to fiddle with the lock.

"I've told you," she said, "no one could open that, not even your granda—"

The cuff sprang open. Darius rushed off to find a loo.

It was ages before he came back, but when he

did he had a huge smile of relief on his face.

Nat was very cross. "If you could always get us out of that, why the flip didn't you?" she said.

Darius looked over at his Grandad Fingers.

Nat didn't understand.

"Family," said Darius with a shrug. "Grandad couldn't do it, so…"

Of course! Nat got it. His grandad could never break out of the cuffs, and so Darius didn't want to show him up!

Every so often, the total and utter chimp that was Darius Bagley did something that made Nat want to hug him. She never did, of course, because he was basically rank, but right then she at least felt the urge.

Nat looked at her watch. "Dad, time's nearly up. Let's do cake here, then get back for Tiffannee's first dance."

As if on cue, Mr Posnitch came over and said to Nat, "Your waiters are bringing the cake out now."

Waiters? thought Nat. *What waiters?*

Three men in tuxedos and bow ties wheeled in Grammy Bagley's cake.

Nat didn't care what Bad News Nan said – Grammy Bagley could make a wonderful-looking wedding cake.

Everyone whooped and cheered at the sight.

There was nothing 'new-age' or 'magic cauldron' about this bit of the wedding. It was a stone-cold wedding cake classic – three snow-white tiers, each delicately balanced on pillars of crystallised sugar, and piped with pink and white roses. The cake seemed to hang suspended in the air, magically floating on columns of ice.

It was perfect.

It was so perfect that everyone stood and applauded. Grammy Bagley shuffled to her feet. She slurred her words a bit, and Nat guessed that those flasks hadn't contained tea.

"You're a rotten lot," she said, "there's hardly a decent one among you. But you're family. And today our family is a bit bigger, and a whole lot better."

Blimey, thought Nat, *these Bagleys are full of surprises*.

"I ain't got no money to give Fiona and Oswald, but I hope they know this cake comes with love."

Fiona started sniffing. "It's beautiful," she said, "thank you."

Oswald stood up. His usually stony face wore an odd expression Nat couldn't recognise. He cleared his throat. He was going to make a speech!

Just then, one of the waiters tripped up, and very nearly fell head-first into the cake.

"OH MY!" the waiter shouted. "Look what very nearly happened."

"WATCH OUT!" shouted the second waiter, grabbing the top tier of the cake as if to move it out of the way, "you're SO CLUMSY. That was nearly a total disaster."

The third waiter started making thrashing movements as he lifted the second tier. "Who put itching powder in my trousers today?" he said. "That's going to make things really difficult."

The guests stared at the three idiots, dismantling the precious cake.

And Nat realised who the waiters were.

They were the comedy waiters Dad had booked for Tiffannee's wedding. And they were starting their rubbish act.

Noooo, she thought, *not here, not now…*

And not the cake.

The precious cake of Grammy Bagley love.

There was a low growl coming from the guests, who were looking at the scene with growing anger. Nat moved towards the waiters to warn them, but she was too late.

The growling noise must have made one of the trio nervous, and when one of the Bagley kids, hyper on sweeties and fizzy pop, shot across the floor in front of him, he tripped for real. The top tier of the cake spun out of his hands, twirled in the air and landed intact, though with a wet splat, on the ground.

Nothing happened for a second.

"That was a close one!" said the clumsy waiter.

Then, like a delayed reaction, all the icing cracked and the cake fell to bits on the floor.

"Oh no, look what I've done!" said the waiter. Nat realised he was being deadly serious.

"It doesn't matter," another waiter hissed, "go with it, keep in character, we're *supposed* to be clumsy, remember? That's the act."

"Yeah, c'mon Quentin," said the other comedy waiter, "remember that everyone will forgive us if we make them laugh."

Oh dear, thought Nat, *that's what my dad thinks*.

AND IT'S STUPID AND WRONG AND ALWAYS ENDS BADLY.

What happened next was stupid and wrong and ended very badly too.

The Bagleys were already furious that Grammy Bagley's wonderful cake was being chucked about and they were about to get even more furious.

The head waiter, the one who thought he was the most hilarious, picked up a chunk of broken cake and deliberately slipped over, sending the cake whizzing over his head.

Where it landed – smack on Oswald Bagley's face.

"Run!" yelled Dad, grabbing Darius and Nat and making a dash for it, just before the place erupted.

"Dad, I could properly murder you and I'm not even joking," hissed Nat, "this is another total disaster."

"Look on the bright side," said Dad, glancing back from the door to see plates, glasses, tables and comedy waiters being hurled about the room, "at least no one's going to notice we've gone."

Outside, the weather had turned as ugly and fierce as the wedding party had inside. Nat, along with Dad, Darius and Bad News Nan (one hand clutching her huge hat firmly to her head, the other just as firmly holding onto a big gloopy piece of cake), fought through tearing winds and lashing rain. They struggled across the car park towards the van.

And there, leaning against the Atomic Dustbin, lit by bolts of lightning, hair streaming in the wind, standing tall and terrifying in the teeth of the storm, stood a lone figure.

Dad make a tiny noise in the back of his throat.

Nat thought it sounded like a prehistoric wombat, running into a peckish, smiling T-Rex. A noise that meant the doomed furry creature had realised that mammals might well be on the winning side one day… but that day was not today.

"Hello love," squeaked Dad.

It was Mum.

WAY more terrifying than that peckish T-Rex.

And she wasn't even smiling.

CHAPTER TWENTY-SEVEN

. . . .

THEY DROVE THROUGH THE GATHERING STORM IN silence for a while.

Eventually Mum said: "Let's make sure I've got this correct. I leave you in charge for a few days and you give Tiffannee's lovely, beautifully planned, super-perfect posh wedding to the massed hordes of Ghenghis Bagley. At the same time, you put our family in an old circus tent and feed them doggy-munched stew. Have I left anything out?"

"Um," said Dad, not taking his eyes off the road.

"Yeah, you've left loads out," said Darius, truthfully. "It's a lot worse than that. You haven't even got to us nobbling all the bridesmaids yet, or losing the rings, or kidnapping a Norwegian tourist, or letting the worst circus in the country loose on them."

"Some of it might have been my fault," said Nat, bravely, hoping a quick confession might reduce her punishment.

"Really? Well I'll come to you later, young lady," said Mum. Nat put her head in her hands.

"Looking on the bright side..." began Dad, but he ended with a strangulated: "Nnnnng." Nat guessed Mum was doing something painful in the front seat.

"Stop-op op that, love," said Dad, "let me faaa-finish. Looking on the bright side, we've almost got through the day and neither Tiffannee or Oswald know about the mix-up. Nat's been a perfect bridesmaid twice over oh AND – and this is a biggie – everyone married the right person!

I call that winning!"

Nat could only see the back of Mum's head. It was shaking, violently.

She's actually going to explode, thought Nat, genuinely scared. *Dad has finally made Mum's head explode, oh heck.*

There was a strange strangled noise from mum. Nat was terrified.

"Ivor Winstanley Cuthbert Bumole," she said, "you are without doubt the most utterly useless human being I have met in my life, ever."

"But he is the funniest," said Darius, simply.

Mum didn't say anything.

Nat felt a familiar surge of affection for her chimp-like friend, followed by the familiar urge of revulsion when she saw just how deep up his nostrils he could get his fingers.

The storm, however, was no laughing matter. Rain was beating down relentlessly now, and by the time they reached the marquée, wind was whipping around the tent ropes and making them whistle and moan scarily.

As they ran out of the van, Nat noted that the ground was already muddy and waterlogged. Her heavy boots were almost sucked into the mud and her fairy wings were limp and soggy. The others headed for the big top as she ducked into the fortune teller's tent to check on the cake.

"Not ready, go away!" yelled Uncle Ernie. "You can't rush art!"

"That's what I told my art teacher," Nat muttered to herself on the way back to the marquée, "but she just gave me a detention."

Inside, the circus folk were taking a bow and the guests were clapping.

All the guests, that is, who weren't putting out little fires, clearing up Buster the rescue dog's poop, comforting the unfunny clowns, finding lost playing cards or trying to untangle the contortionist.

Nat saw that Tiffannee and Hiram were just sitting, open-mouthed.

"I'll go say hello," said Mum, "carry on with your plan meanwhile. Apparently, you've got everything under control in your own way."

"Cake's not ready," Nat said to Dad as soon as Mum was out of earshot.

"We need to get the disco started," said Dad, handing Darius his music player, "then no one will be able to hear the howling storm outside, or realise there's no cake yet."

Tiffannee ran over and hugged Mum when she saw her.

"And how is – everything?" asked Mum, pointedly.

Nat, eavesdropping nearby, cringed as she heard Tiffannee admit it had been "different." She saw Mum frown.

"VERY different," said Chief Bridesmaid Daisy Wetwipe as she walked past sniffily.

"You'll find that's like marriage," Mum said to Tiffannee, looking at Dad. "It's very different to what you plan. But…" her voice softened a little – "but it doesn't mean it's worse."

"I go home now?" said Henrik Henriksonn, popping up at that moment. His hair was singed. You stood too close to the fireeater, thought Nat, silly man.

"No," said Mum, firmly, "more pictures, snap away."

Just then, Nat spotted her teacher, Miss Hunny, looking pretty but nervous in a long silver dress. Hiram's best man smiled at her, and offered her a glass of bubbly.

Miss Hunny being here can only mean one thing, thought Nat.

King Ivor and the Hunnypots.

Time seemed to go into slow motion, like in a horror-filled dream. How could she have forgotten – the worst was yet to come.

Dad – was – tuning – his – ukulele!

Nooooooo.

Nat cringed – they were actually going to perform after Darius had 'warmed up' the audience.

Within minutes, techno-genius Darius had set up the sound system and had begun to DJ.

Nat suddenly remembered what music Darius liked. She ran to Dad and tugged at his sleeve.

"Are you totally sure about this?" she said. "Only there could be several aunties and uncles about to learn a LOT of new words. And I don't want to see Nan twerking."

"Don't worry," said Dad, "you're a terrible one for worrying."

But Darius didn't play any of *his* favourite songs. At that moment he put on a PROPERLY SOPPY ONE. Tiffannee and Hiram's favourite.

"*Our love is perfect*," sang the sappy singer, "*'cos we've got perfect love*."

Vom-tastic, thought Nat.

But Tiffannee and Hiram smiled at each other and walked out on to the makeshift dance floor for the first dance. A glitter ball sparkled shafts of light across the tent and the newly-weds, eyes only for each other, began a slow, smoochy dance.

Everyone applauded.

"You might, somehow, get away with this," Mum said to Dad, as she joined them both, "unlikely as it seems."

Dad smiled his idiot goofy smile. Mum burst out laughing.

"Come here, you big dope," she said, her whole body shaking, "I've been trying not to laugh for an hour, but it's impossible."

Dad hugged Mum. They both dashed over and hugged Tiffannee and Hiram, who looked puzzled.

"Know this, Tiffannee, if your daft husband gives you as much joy as mine, you'll be the happiest woman alive."

"Does that mean I'm not in trouble?" asked Dad, hopefully, as they strolled back towards Nat.

"No, you're in massive trouble," said Mum, but she kissed him as she said it.

Repelled as Nat was by this, she breathed a sigh of relief. For the first time since the weddings had started, she felt a surge of hope.

They had totally rescued the weddings!

And then the storm blew the marquée away.

CHAPTER TWENTY-EIGHT

. . . .

IT WAS SO QUICK, NO ONE WAS REALLY SURE HOW it happened.

One minute the bride and groom were smooching under a disco ball, the next they were standing in a soggy, rain-lashed field.

The guests all screamed and ran for cover as all the ropes on one side of the big top seemed to give way and the gale caught the underside of the tent and flipped it over.

Nat noticed that Mum managed to tread on Dad's ukulele in the chaos AND make it look accidental

It went *crunch*.

"Ooopsie," said Mum, as the neck snapped. Dad looked horror-struck, Miss Hunny looked relieved.

"AAAARGH!" said Tiffannee's dad, zooming past, holding on to a tent rope and trying to pull it downwards. He lost his footing and was dragged, face down, through the mud.

"I'll help you," shouted Dad, and ran after him.

"Can I go home *now*?" shouted Henrik Henriksonn, who was tangled up in a tent rope and dragging along behind him.

Guests ran for their cars. They tried to drive off but the soft ground was so muddy, their wheels just turned uselessly. They were all stuck.

"Into the caravans!" shouted Darius, and the guests scrambled and ran for the empty circus vans.

Tiffannee ran in little circles in the middle of the chaos. Her dress was totally ruined. Her crown of wildflowers was sliding colourfully down her face, and her beautiful shoes were plastered in mud.

Her bottom lip trembled as she looked around at the ruins of her big day.

Chief Bridesmaid Daisy Wetwipe stood in the middle of the field, cackling. She looked like a witch, summoning a storm. She grabbed hold of Tiffannee, as Hiram ducked for shelter in a caravan.

"SHE'S done this!" screamed Daisy Wetwipe pointing at Nat, her limp, soggy fairy wings quivering with rage. "It's all Nathalia's fault. She's sabotaged us because she couldn't be Chief Fairy Princess Bridesmaid. I told you so!"

Nathalia just stood there, soaked and miserable.

Tiffannee looked at Nat with a look of hurt and anger. It was horrible.

Nat looked at the soaked bride splattered with mud. Daisy was right, in a way. She HAD ruined her cousin's big day. She felt ashamed of herself.

And then a tent peg fell out of Daisy's purse.

Nat and Tiffannee gasped.

Tiffannee bent down to pick it up.

"You pulled this out?" she said to Daisy, holding up the tent peg. "You DELIBERATELY SABOTAGED my wedding. In the middle of my first dance!

The chief bridesmaid was lost for words. Her make-up ran down her face in the rain, making her look like one of the sad clowns. Just then Henrik Henrikson popped up and took a photo of her.

"And worst of all," yelled Tiffannee, "then you tried to blame it on my own *family*?"

"I can explain…" said Daisy, desperately. She pointed at Nat. "It's all her fault. She's mad with jealousy. She got rid of the other bridesmaids and now she's planted this tent peg on me. She's still trying to get rid of me, even if it means ruining your wedding. It's called bridesmaid fever!"

Tiffannee strode over to the rambling bridesmaid and snatched her soggy crown of flowers from her head.

"Oh do shut up, you AWFUL woman," snapped Tiffannee.

Nat and Darius grabbed Tiffannee's arm and led the sodden bride into the first caravan they saw.

The three of them dried themselves on some handy blankets and shawls.

"I guess this makes you my Chief Bridesmaid," said Tiffannee, with a smile, handing over the head-dress. But it was a sad smile.

Nat had to admit the bride looked a bit down.

"Not gone perfectly, has it?" said Nat. "I'm ever so sorry."

"It's not that that's making me sad." Tiffannee's lip trembled. "The thing is," she said, "girls spend years and years thinking about their wedding."

I won't, thought Nat, *unless its years of thinking about how to avoid it.*

"And every magazine you read, and everyone on telly and all your friends say it has to be perfect, the most perfect day of your life."

Nat put a comforting arm around her.

"It made me bonkers," said Tiffannee, "Nevermind bridesmaid fever, I've had bridal insanity! I even made you un-invite lovely Uncle Ernie. What was I thinking? I wish he was here so I could say sorry." She sniffed, unhappily: "I must be the worst bride *ever*."

Nat didn't know what to say. She pulled off her fairy wings, miserably

Everything was ruined and she felt terrible.

Until the door opened.

And in came Hiram the groom, Mum, the two dads, the two nans and the FBI men, followed by un-uninvited Uncle Ernie (with his rescue dog Buster)...

Ernie was wheeling in:

The most genuinely, astonishingly amazing cake Nat had ever seen.

It was a cake that even her made-up pretend chef Marcel would have been proud of.

Instead of a boring, remodelled, ordinary

wedding cake, there stood:

Beautiful cake models of the bride and groom!

Tiffannee couldn't speak.

Everyone burst into wild applause.

"I'd had so much practice making the matchstick gnomes," Uncle Ernie said, "that this was a doddle."

Gnomes? Raymonde mouthed to Dad, who indicated he'd explain later.

"OMG, Uncle Ernie, that's AMAZING!" said Tiffannee. She embraced Ernie, who trouser-trumped with pride. "After what I did, you must really love me to still have made these?!"

"We all love you, hon," said Hiram.

Tiffannee blubbered – this time, happily.

Uncle Ernie grinned from wonky ear to ear. Buster ran round his legs in happy doggy circles.

"I'm SO sorry about the invite," said Tiffannee, with tears in her eyes. Nat didn't know if the tears were because of her emotion or because of the smelly trump.

"And I'm so sorry to you, Nat," said Tiffannee giving her a hug. "I know being a Fairy Princess with those other awful bridesmaids wasn't exactly fun…"

Nat smiled. "Nah, I totally get it now. Weddings are about family. And sometimes family are daft and embarrassing. And sometimes they even make you dress like Esmerelda the spanner fairy…" She took a deep breath and said, with total honesty, "but it's been an honour to be your bridesmaid Tiff, thank you so much for asking me." Dad hugged Nat, the soppy idiot.

Tiffannee broke into a big teary-eyed smile. Her face lit up and it was like the sun peeking out from a raincloud.

"You know," said the bride, cuddling up to Raymonde, "my dad's here, I married the man I love and I'm surrounded by people who actually, properly care for me."

"That's true," said Nat, shouting over the rain hammering on the caravan roof.

"I wanted today to be perfect. But it doesn't matter any more that my wedding hasn't gone according to plan. This IS sort-of perfect."

"Yeah, sort-of perfect," said Nat. She heard yells from outside the van. She looked out of the window at the trapped wedding guests, desperately trying to get their cars out of the muddy swamp.

"That works for me," said Tiffannee. "I've had a sort-of perfect wedding. It's just a shame my family didn't get the party I promised them."

And then an INCREDIBLE thought struck Nat.

"Chimpy," she said, pinching Darius to get his attention, "have you got Fiona's mobile number?"

She dialled the new bride. "Fiona," said Nat, "you know you said we're family now? And you know the way that family always helps each other out...?"

Nat turned to Tiffannee. "Stand by, your family's about to get a whole lot bigger," she said, with a grin.

CHAPTER TWENTY-NINE

• • • •

NAT RECKONED THE RESCUE OPERATION THAT TOOK place over the following hour was noisier and messier and windier than Bad News Nan on Boxing Day.

It was a bit like a film she had seen about the escape from the Dunkirk beaches but instead of hundreds of little ships, there were loads of rubbish cars roaring up to the stranded wedding guests, headlights blazing, with ropes and chains and hairy, shouty Bagleys.

There were enough Bagleys who *didn't* drink

to drive the cars, and enough Bagleys who DID drink, not to mind hauling vehicles out of the mud. In fact, they seemed to think it was a great wedding hoot!

"It's nice to be the hero sometimes," Fingers Bagley said to Nat, as he yanked on a rope.

A blue light flashed. "Oh heck," said the old safe-cracker. It was the police.

But they were here to help too.

It was Fiona's mates from the local station. "The town was very quiet," explained Sergeant Nabber, hopping out of his car, "probably because all the troublemakers are here," he muttered, looking around.

One by one, the trapped cars were hauled out of the swampy ground. The only thing totally stuck was Dad's pride and joy – the Atomic Dustbin.

"We'll have to abandon her, Dad," shouted Nat in the teeth of the gale.

But then a roar split the air. It was new bride

PC Fiona Bagley – and she was on Oswald's favourite, most powerful, biggest bike.

The Beast.

"I thought he'd dismantled it to make your wedding rings," Nat shouted to Fiona, as Oswald attached a heavy towing chain to Dad's van. Fiona showed Nat her empty hand. Her ring was gone!

"I said he could put the engine bits together for this rescue," she said, "so I guess he's got his rotten bike back. Oh well, nothing's perfect is it?

"Tell me about it!" said Nat.

"At least I get to ride it now," yelled Fiona, happily.

With a roar and a screech and a big sucking sound, The Beast pulled the Atomic Dustbin clear of the mud.

Tiffannee walked up to the triumphant Fiona.

She was by now looking like a drowned fairy queen. Fiona giggled, and Tiffannee put an arm around her. "I think we're going to get on very well," she said.

"Everyone back to the Country Club!" shouted Fiona. "We're having a party!"

And WHAT a party.

By midnight, the joint wedding bash was clearly a massive, a roaring, a gigantic, a *perfect* success.

Darius's DJ set was totally banging. It was so good he got EVERYONE dancing, even Bad News Nan.

Who didn't twerk, hoorah.

Unlike Grammy Bagley, aaaargh.

Penny even persuaded Nat to get up and dance and Mr Posnitch taught them the famous Albanian Two-Step Tango.

New groom Hiram was line-dancing with new bride Fiona, and new groom Oswald was twirling new bride Tiffannee over his head like a cane.

Fiona's police chums were arm-wrestling with the FBI agents to prove who were the better crime-fighters. The FBI men won the arm-wrestling, but then realised they'd lost Raymonde! They wanted to chase after him but Oswald gently convinced them to stay a bit longer.

Fingers Bagley and Fiona's grandad had got roaring drunk and Nat watched as they began sobbing on each others' shoulders, saying how sorry they were to have been enemies for so long.

"This is better than perfect," yelled Tiffannee, as Oswald whizzed her about again, "you're the best, Nat."

Yeah, I must be pretty good, organising all this, thought Nat, feeling pleased with herself for the first time for AGES.

Mum danced up to Nat, "You do realise you're turning into your father?" she said. "He makes a total pig's ear of things but everyone still loves him. It drives me nuts."

"I'd rather be you, Mum," said Nat, alarmed and feeling less pleased with herself, but Mum just laughed and twirled Nat around.

"Where IS your daft dad?" Mum went on. "I

haven't seen him for a while, which makes me nervous."

"That's how I feel about Darius," said Nat, and Mum laughed again.

Suddenly the music stopped. Everyone booed. Then Nat saw them, walking up to the stage. It was Dad, dressed in a too-tight gold jacket, and Miss Hunny in her pretty dress. She was carrying a mike, Dad was carrying a ukulele with the neck sellotaped back on.

"Oh no," said Mum, "not this, anything but this."

Nat felt faint. It had all been going so well…

Dad took the mike.

"I'm very sorry but King Ivor and The Hunnypots have split up over musical differences," he said. Though he was smiling.

Everyone who had ever heard Dad play, cheered.

"Basically, I've been chucked out of my own band," said Dad, to more cheering.

With a smile he handed his uke to Hiram's best man, Mike J Stenkowitz Jr, who strummed it expertly.

Mike and Miss Hunny took to the stage and something rather wonderful happened.

They were flipping brilliant. Miss Hunny had a voice like an angel dipped in – well, honey – and Mike played the ukulele in a way Nat had never heard before – that is, in tune and in time.

They played three of Tiffannee and Hiram's favourite songs and everyone joined in on the choruses.

Then they played one of Oswald's favourite songs and everyone put their fingers in their ears.

"He's a tiny bit better than me," said Dad, standing next to Nat. Nat squeezed his hand, gratefully.

"Plus," said Dad kindly, "I reckoned you might have suffered enough embarrassment today already."

This time he got a proper hug.

It was almost dawn when the joint wedding party finally broke up and the last remaining guests staggered out into clean, fresh morning air, all storm clouds long since blown away.

Everyone agreed it had been the best wedding – the best WEDDINGS – ever.

Tons of lovely things happened.

The local paper was going to run a story about the heroic Bagleys and ensure they were allowed to party in the town again.

Henrik Henriksonn didn't win the church picture prize, but he did get his photos of the dramatic rescue published in the local paper. Which made Peter Petersonn green with envy.

Plus, his pictures of Uncle Ernie's cake got Uncle Ernie a new career as a celebrity baker.

Tiffannee's escaped dad Raymonde still keeps in touch with regular postcards from Mexico.

Mr Posnitch fell in love with the tangled-up contortionist from the circus.

Daisy Wetwipe left the country in shame.

Miss Hunny and Mike the best man formed a new band and made a record.

Bad News Nan and Grammy Bagley discovered they both loved funerals and promised to share any future invites, to double the fun.

And both Fiona AND Tiffannee told Nat she was the greatest bridesmaid in the history of bridesmaids, just before slipping away with their new husbands, and that GROWN UP look on their faces.

Yuk.

A pink dawn slid across the horizon as Uncle Spiro plopped a sleepy Darius in the back of his car.

"See ya, chimpy," said Nat.

"Not if I see you first, Buttface," said Darius.

"He's staying with us for a week," said the circus-master, "he's got some great ideas for our next show. Ninja nightmares, he calls it, could be a winner."

The driver, one of the miserable clowns, pulled away.

They got about six feet before the wheels fell

off and the top sprang open and custard squirted out of the engine.

"Oops – it's the clown's car," said Spiro. "I forgot."

Finally, only Nat, Mum and Dad were left. They stood happily outside the Country Club, waiting for a cab. Nat was shattered, but full of a warm glow inside. Job done, she thought, yawning, somehow...

"Forgot to mention," said Dad, "my cousin Isobel got engaged at the party. She's had a great time. She's asked if Nat would be her Chief Bridesmaid and if I'd be her wedding planner."

Nat looked at Mum.

"Obviously I said yes," said Dad.

Mum and Nat chased him around the car park with his broken ukulele.

The End

Have you read...?

Nat has a chance to start afresh at a new school,
in a new town… but with the same old embarrassing
dad. Uh-oh! This isn't going to end well…

Summer holidays are here and Nat's off to the
South of France. Surely even embarrassing
Dad can't ruin this? Don't bet on it!

When a video of Nat dancing goes viral she soon
realises fame isn't all it's cracked up to be…
Especially with THE MOST EMBARRASSING
DAD IN THE WORLD as a manager!